"Don't tak   **e a lot smarter**   **for."**

Equal parts furi
at him for all sh
possibly take tha

Men misjudged her all the time, to the point where she'd actually resigned herself to it. To most of them, she was nothing more than a pretty accessory on their arm, something they wore like a designer watch to make them look good. That Ben had seen past her appearance to her intelligence pleased her immensely. If she hadn't been so mad at him, she'd have complimented him for his perceptiveness.

Giving her a sheepish look, he took a step forward. Then another. He was getting close to violating her comfort zone, but she planted her feet and met his gaze without flinching. Cocking his head, he gave her a slow, approving grin. "I don't scare you anymore, do I?"

"You never did."

"Who was he?"

The blunt question caught her off guard, and she blinked in surprise. "Who was who?"

"The guy who made you afraid," he clarified in an understanding voice. "The one who made you run away."

MIA ROSS

loves great stories. She enjoys reading about fascinating people, long-ago times and exotic places. But only for a little while, because her reality is pretty sweet. Married to her college sweetheart, she's the proud mom of two amazing kids, whose schedules keep her hopping. Busy as she is, she can't imagine trading her life for anyone else's—and she has a pretty good imagination. You can visit her online at www.miaross.com.

Seaside Romance

Mia Ross

Recycling programs for this product may not exist in your area.

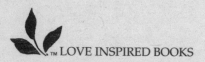

™ LOVE INSPIRED BOOKS

ISBN-13: 978-0-373-81752-8

SEASIDE ROMANCE

Copyright © 2014 by Andrea Chermak

www.Harlequin.com

Printed in U.S.A.

And the light shineth in darkness.
—*John* 1:5

For my friends
who found the courage to leave the past behind.

Acknowledgments

To the very talented folks who help me make my
books everything they can be: Elaine Spencer,
Melissa Endlich and the dedicated staff
at Love Inspired.

More thanks to the gang at Seekerville
(www.seekerville.net). It's a great place
to hang out with readers—and writers!

I've been blessed with a wonderful network
of supportive, encouraging family and friends.
You inspire me every day!

Chapter One

"Oh, no." Kneeling in front of the box she'd just opened full of stuffed animals, Lauren Foster groaned. "All these Easter bunnies are green."

"That's okay," her friend Julia Stanton assured her without looking over. "I ordered lots of green ones."

"This kind of green?" Lauren held up a little hopper that was completely adorable—except for the fact that he was the color of a lime highlighter.

Julia glanced down and shuddered. "Definitely not. There must be some kind of mix-up with the supplier. What does the shipping label say?"

Angling her head, Lauren read, "Toylane, 64 Main Street, Oakbridge, Maine."

"That's happened before. I guess I should

have researched other toy stores in the area before picking the name Toyland," she added with a light laugh.

"Since I'm watching the store while you and Nick are on your honeymoon, I should probably learn how to handle things like this. What do you want me to do?"

In reply, Julia extended a graceful hand sporting the most gorgeous diamond setting Lauren had ever seen. She'd been in Holiday Harbor with her old friend all weekend, and seeing that ring on her left hand still astounded Lauren. Just last month, she'd been trying on jewelry like that, living in a luxury apartment overlooking Central Park and shopping her way from one upscale boutique to another.

What a difference a week makes, she thought bitterly.

When she realized Julia was still waiting for the invoice, Lauren slid it from its clear sleeve and handed it over. "Sorry. Blanked out there for a minute."

Julia gave her an understanding smile. "Running a toy store isn't as easy as it looks, so you're forgiven."

Lauren congratulated herself on evading the real reason she was so distracted. She hadn't told anyone why she left New York in such a hurry, and she wanted to keep it that way as long as humanly possible. Maybe forever.

When her text alert chimed, she glanced down to find a message from her mother.

Have a great day, sweetie—xo.

After texting back u 2, Lauren swiveled to look over at Julia. "I love my parents, but I wish they could remember I'm twenty-eight years old."

Julia laughed. "My parents used to be like that, too."

"How'd you get them to stop?"

"I came here and started my own business. Then I met Nick, and you know the rest."

Her dreamy smile clearly said she'd found someone to love for the rest of her life, and Lauren was ashamed to admit she was envious. Not that she begrudged Julia her happiness, but she wanted some of it for herself. Sadly, she was further from it now than she'd ever been. Personally and professionally, her life was in pieces, and she had no idea how to put it back together.

Shoving her negative attitude aside, she focused on Julia. They'd known each other since college, and she was the kind of friend who didn't ask Lauren why she needed to run away.

Instead, she'd opened up her home and offered Lauren a job for as long as she wanted it.

"When you first sent me pictures of this place last summer," she said while she opened a box holding a fleet of cars and trucks, "I thought you were nuts to move up here so far from civilization. Now I see why you like it so much."

"It's out of the way, that's for sure, but that's what I like most about it." Looking away from the computer screen, she added a warm smile. "It's been so much fun having you here. How long has it been?"

After a moment, Lauren replied, "Five years ago, Mom and I met you and your mother in Paris for Fashion Week."

"Oh, I remember that. I still have the clothes I bought on that trip. They're a little outdated, but they're so beautiful I don't have the heart to get rid of them."

"If you just wait a few years, they'll come back in style."

They both laughed, and Julia said, "I should get in touch with this supplier to make sure the bunnies I actually ordered are on their way. I have the number in my office, so I'll call from there. Can you handle customers alone for a few minutes?"

"Sure," Lauren responded with more confidence than she felt. Then again, she thought, as she carried the box over to restock the vehicles section, these days she pretty much did everything with more bravado than she felt. When the rug got yanked out from under your life, you kept going as best you could.

The bells along the top of the entry door jingled, and she called out, "Be with you in a minute!"

"Take your time. I'm not in a hurry."

The words weren't the least bit threatening, but the unfamiliar male voice froze her midstep. Although her brain knew perfectly well she was protected behind the tall shelves, her heart thudded to a stop, and icy fear slithered up her spine. Pulling in a ragged breath, she reminded herself that no one but her parents knew she was in Northern Maine with Julia.

You're safe now, a tiny voice in her mind whispered. Closing her eyes, she took another, calmer breath and braced herself to face her very first customer. She plastered a smile on her face and walked out from behind the shelves. "May I help you?"

He flashed her a bright grin that made her feel as if he'd been waiting all morning to meet her. "You must be Julia's friend Lauren, from New York City. Last time I was in, she told me you were coming to help out with the shop." Offering his hand, he added, "I'm Ben Thomas. Welcome to Holiday Harbor."

The name sounded vaguely familiar, but she couldn't place it. Dressed in washed-out jeans and work boots, he stood a full head taller than her, and Lauren had to tilt her head up to get a full view of him. With windblown blond hair and a ruddy complexion, he looked like he'd just stepped off one of the fishing boats docked down at the wharf. Then it occurred to her where she knew that name from, and she looked down at the top of the antique glass-front case Julia used as a checkout stand. Like the rest of the wood in the shop, from display racks to molding, it was a rich, dark walnut, obviously hand-carved with care a long time ago.

A shiny brass nameplate mounted near the front of the cabinet read "Restored with pride by Ben Thomas," and she tapped it with her fingertip. "Is this you?"

"Yeah. When Julia was gutting this place, we found it upstairs in a corner, in a dozen pieces and covered with—well, you get the picture."

He smiled again, and she couldn't help noticing that the faded blue T-shirt he wore paled in comparison to his eyes. The color of a flaw-less summer sky, they made her think of sunshine. There hadn't been much of that for her recently, and even though she'd just met him, she sensed herself being drawn to the warmth he projected. As the pause continued, she realized he was expecting some kind of response from her.

Nodding, she said, "I think so."

"Anyway, she had a vision for this place, wanted to restore it to the way it used to be. It was built as a general store, and I dug up old blueprints and photos to make sure we got it right. I thought using the original counter would be a nice way to keep the old character in her new shop. It took a while, and when I was done, she insisted I get credit for it. Thanks to her, I've gotten some jobs restoring antiques for other folks in town."

A man who saw value in old, broken-down things and enjoyed resurrecting them, she thought with a little smile. It was quite a departure from the bulldoze-the-past mentality so many people had these days. "So you're not just a contractor. You're a craftsman."

"I'd like to be. There's tons of old places along the East Coast that need to be saved. Bringing them back to life would be the best job ever."

"Why don't you do it?"

Annoyance clouded his expression, but blew

away as quickly as it had surfaced. "Thomas and Sons is just me and my dad these days. Kitchens and roofs aren't my idea of exciting, but they pay the bills. Without me—"

He shrugged, but she got the drift. He was staying here, forgoing his own dreams to help his father. It was a sweet, considerate thing to do, and she smiled in spite of herself. "That's really great of you, staying to make sure his business keeps running well."

"That's what family's all about, but thanks."

His gaze warmed with the kind of male admiration she used to crave, but now it sent her skittering back from the counter. Lauren had learned the hard way that people weren't always what they seem. Sometimes their true natures were buried beneath layers of deception, and by the time you dug deep enough to discover the truth, it was almost impossible to claw your way back out.

Determined not to repeat her mistakes, Lauren resolved to be pleasant to Ben but keep a respectable distance. "So, what can I help you with?"

Either he didn't notice her sudden back-pedaling routine, or he didn't care. Whatever the reason, he sailed along without skipping a beat. "Julia called to say the puzzles I ordered for my niece's birthday are here. I came to add a card so she can ship them to Detroit for me."

"Ben!" Hurrying out front, Julia set the phone on the counter near the register and embraced him with enthusiasm. "I haven't seen you in ages. How are things?"

"Fine. How 'bout you?"

"Crazy, with Easter next week and the wedding a month away." Laughing as if chaos was her normal mode, she added, "Your gift is in the back, wrapped and ready to go. You two chat while I get it."

"I can—" Lauren's protest was lost in a graceful pirouette that sent her friend toward the storeroom. Stranded with Ben, she did her best to shrug it off. "She's the boss."

"Yeah, that's what her fiancé says, too." He chuckled. "Never figured he'd let someone take over his life that way, but he seems really happy."

"So does Julia," Lauren said. Not long ago, she'd been adept at mingling and making small talk with people she'd just met. Now, though, it terrified her to even try. Just one more thing she had to overcome, she groused silently.

Apparently, her discomfort was pretty obvious, because Ben leaned across the counter with a sympathetic expression. "This map-dot town's not exactly what you're used to, huh?"

Thankful that he hadn't guessed the true source of her shyness, she shook her head. "It's nice, though. It was so pretty driving in past the lighthouse and seeing the village spread out over the coast that way. With all these old buildings and houses, it feels like it's been here forever."

"Founded on Christmas Day, 1820," he confirmed. "That's where the name came from, and some of the original families are still here. I imagine they'll still be around a hundred years from now."

She caught a hint of disapproval in his tone, and the light in his eyes dimmed slightly. "You make that sound like a bad thing."

"When you stay in one place too long, you stagnate, like a pond. Life needs to move from one place to another like the tide, to keep things interesting."

Just then, Julia returned with Ben's package, wrapped in festive birthday paper and topped with a poufy pink bow.

"Looks great. Thanks."

Taking it from her, he handed over his credit card and easily shifted to a conversation about her upcoming wedding. He politely included Lauren, but she was only half listening. Instead, her mind was churning around his very down-to-earth philosophy on how to avoid a stagnant life. Maybe that was what she needed, Lauren mused while she rang up his purchase. A fresh start, with a few waves for variety.

The problem was, while it sounded appealing, she knew she wasn't ready for anything quite that ambitious yet. Right now, she needed a safe harbor. Eventually, once she regained all the parts of her she'd lost over the past year, she could think about venturing a little farther from shore.

A voice came from the phone, and Julia cradled it against her shoulder. *"T-o-y-l-a-n-d,"* she spelled in the perfect diction Lauren had always admired. "The label says, *T-o-y-l-a-n-e.* Yes, I'll hold."

Rolling her eyes, she smiled at him. "I hope your niece likes them."

"Yeah, me, too." He winked at Lauren as she returned his card. "You know how girls are. They say they want one thing when they really want something else."

She knew he was joking, but the comment struck her the wrong way, and she glared up at him. "I have no idea what you're talking about."

Her scolding had no effect on him whatsoever, and he gave her a maddening grin. "My mistake."

The other line rang, and Lauren picked up

the handset. "Toyland, this is Lauren. May I help you?" After a moment, she said, "Okay. We'll be there in a few minutes."

Still on hold, Julia gave her a questioning look.

"The sandwich and cookie trays you ordered for the Easter egg coloring party are ready at the bakery. They're taking up a lot of space in the cooler, so they'd like us to get them ASAP."

"Oh, no! I forgot all about them. The first set of kids and their parents will be here in half an hour." Julia cast a pleading look at Ben. "The platters aren't heavy, but there's three of them, and they're huge. Could you possibly help us out?"

Us? Considering the inexplicable reaction she'd had to him earlier, Lauren knew she shouldn't spend any more time with the friendly contractor than absolutely necessary. "I can manage, Julia. It's not that far, so I'll just make an extra trip."

"No need for that," he assured her with a you-can-count-on-me grin. "I'm always glad to lend a pretty lady a hand."

His open admiration of her was both flattering and terrifying, and Lauren swallowed hard to get control of both emotions before she blurted out something inappropriate. "All right, thanks."

Lame but safe, she decided as they headed for the door. Outside on the sidewalk, he paused between the two large display windows she'd rearranged that morning. "Very nice," he approved with a nod. "If I was a kid, they'd make me want to go inside and see what else is in there."

"That was the idea."

Clearly surprised, he turned to look at her. "Wait, you did this?"

"The Stantons are in London," she explained, "and they called early this morning to talk to Julia about the wedding. She likes to redo the windows every Monday but wasn't going to have time. Since she was busy, I thought I'd take a shot at decorating."

"Great job."

His unexpected praise settled nicely over Lauren's badly bruised ego, and she took a minute to admire her handiwork. One window held all manner of Easter things: baskets, stuffed animals and a sampling of the unique toys the shop kept in stock. The other window framed a miniature version of Holiday Harbor, complete with early nineteenth-century buildings and gardens. In the model town square, tiny children held even tinier baskets filled with packing pellets that resembled eggs.

Even in still life, it was so charming, Lauren easily understood why Julia had chosen to settle here. Maybe someday, she thought wistfully, she'd find a place like this where she could restart her life.

"You okay?" Ben asked, hauling her back to reality.

"Sure." To prove it, she met his concerned gaze with a steady one of her own. With his solid frame and weathered appearance, he made her think of a tree sturdy enough to weather a good old-fashioned hurricane. Pushing the fanciful impression aside, she asked, "Why?"

"You sighed." As if he'd just caught on, he gave her a wry grin. "You want to handle this errand yourself, don't you? So Julia will know you can manage running the shop while she's gone?"

That wasn't quite it, but she'd just met him and confessing that he made her irrationally nervous didn't seem like the right way to go. "No, it's fine. Really," she added with a smile to smooth out the creases in his forehead.

"If you're sure." When she nodded, he motioned her ahead of him. "Then ladies first."

More than once, he'd referred to her as a

lady. Not only that, she mused as she started walking, he actually made her feel like one. She couldn't recall the last time someone had done that for her, and despite her lingering misgivings, she had to admit she liked it.

Lauren Foster was like a Thoroughbred, Ben quickly realized. Beautiful to look at but skittish as anything.

Dressed in conservative gray trousers and a navy blouse, she appeared to be ready for work in an office somewhere. When she turned her head to look across the street, he noticed the way her ponytail caught the sunlight in a cascade of honey-gold curls. It was an intriguing contradiction to the all-business outfit, more suited to a picnic than a job indoors.

Women usually took to him right away, so her standoffish manner baffled him. Then again, he amended as they strolled along, maybe it wasn't him. The idea that someone in her past had done something to make her so timid riled his protective nature, and he had to remind himself it was none of his business. She was Julia's friend, nothing more. Still, he wouldn't mind getting to know her better, figure out what was going on behind those amazing blue eyes.

"Isn't that the church in Julia's model village?" Lauren asked, pointing to the old-fashioned white chapel tucked into the town square.

"The Safe Harbor Church. Pastor McHenry is Julia's future father-in-law, and he'll be doing the ceremony."

"I couldn't believe it when she told me Nick's the son of a preacher. I've read his *Kaleidoscope* magazine online, and in his picture he looks more like the dark, dangerous type."

"Oh, he is," Ben assured her with a laugh. "Except with Julia. She doesn't let him brood too much, which is why she's perfect for him."

"That's nice."

Ben sensed she was less than impressed by his buddy's religious background, but he figured it wouldn't hurt to nudge her a little. "Our pastor's really great, and not intimidating at all. If you wanted to come to Sunday service with Julia, we'd be glad to have you."

Lauren gave him a suspicious once-over. "You go to church?"

"I met Nick in Sunday school." Recalling the early days of their friendship made him grin. They were both twenty-eight now, and they still rarely agreed on anything. "When we were kids, we got in a fight over the best way to build the walls of Jericho."

"Weren't those the ones that came down?" she teased.

That he'd finally gotten this very somber woman to lighten up a little made Ben feel like he'd scored a touchdown. "To be fair, God had a hand in that. It wasn't the masons' fault."

"I guess." Her brief moment of humor evaporated into a frown. "I appreciate the invitation, but religion's really not my thing. We used to go when I was a kid, but now I'm more the sleep-till-noon-go-have-brunch kind of girl."

Ben suspected she could use some of the warmth he always found in the old chapel, but he'd learned long ago that it's impossible to convince someone of something they don't half believe already. You could try, but in the end, you were just wasting your breath.

"That's fine," he said as he pulled open the door to the bakery. "If you change your mind, you know how to get there."

Once inside, Lauren paused and took a deep breath. "Mmm…something smells delicious. What is it?"

"Carolina's snickerdoodles, runner-up at the state fair last summer."

"Carolina? Are they named for the state, or is that someone's name?"

"Carolina and her sister Georgia are from

Alabama, but they've been here ever since I can remember." Affectionately known around town as the Bakery Sisters, they were two of Holiday Harbor's favorite residents. "They came up for a vacation with their husbands and never left. Kinda like Julia."

Lauren gave him an odd look. "I was just thinking the same thing."

"Great minds and all that." Her eyes narrowed, and he tried not to take her reaction personally. Judging by her rapidly shifting moods, something was going on with her, and he opted to cut her some slack. For better or worse, he'd had a lot of practice with that kind of thing. "If you wanna try the snickerdoodles, we should get 'em now. They won't last long."

"That would be great. If they were second place, I can't imagine what came in first."

"Mavis Freeman's gingerbread. She's our lighthouse keeper, and she wins every year."

"I thought all those beacons were automated these days," his guest commented as they joined the line.

"Not the Last Chance Lighthouse," he informed her. "Mavis would strap herself to the tower if we tried to change anything out there."

"Let me guess. It got its name because it's

the last chance a boat has to change course before it crashes on the rocks."

Grinning, he pointed at her. "You got it."

"There seems to be a story for everything in this town. It's interesting."

That was a nice way of putting it, he thought. Growing up, he'd enjoyed living in his quirky hometown, with its salty character and down-to-earth people. Now that he was getting older and still right where he'd started, the age-old traditions were starting to wear on him. Nothing ever changed here, and he knew the villagers inside and out. Maybe that was why Lauren had snared his attention so quickly. Tired of the same old, same old, he was dying to experience something new.

That was it, he decided, relieved to discover the reason for his fascination with her. She was pleasant company, but nothing more than that.

When they arrived at the counter, Georgia Bynes greeted them with a bright, grandmotherly smile. "There's our favorite fix-it man. And you must be Lauren." She reached across the counter to shake hands. "We've heard so much about you. It's wonderful to finally meet you in person. Carolina—" she called out "—Julia's friend is here!"

A slightly younger version of Georgia bustled through the swinging doors, wiping her hands on her flour-dusted apron before echoing her sister's greeting. "Good to see you both. Your trays are ready, so I'll just go get them."

"Don't bother," Ben said, strolling over to the antique cooler that occupied half of the back wall. "I got 'em."

While Lauren signed the delivery receipt, he slid the three trays free and closed the door with his boot. When she appeared behind him with her hands out, he was confused. "What?"

"I can carry at least one."

"They're all balanced and everything. If you just get the door, I'll be fine." She didn't respond, but she didn't drop her hands, either. After a brief standoff, he relented and let her take the top tray from him. "Stubborn, aren't you?"

"Is that a bad thing?"

"Not always." Chuckling, he backed into the entry door to open it for her. "Guess it depends on the situation."

She slanted him a curious look. "What kind of situation makes it bad?"

"Like if you insisted on going into a burning building to save your clothes, I'd have to stop you."

That got him a derisive snort. "Do I look like a moron?"

"Not a bit," he assured her, and was surprised to find he meant it. Normally, he took his time sizing up new people, but this enigmatic woman with the tentative smile had impressed him from the moment he met her. It wasn't just her looks, either. Gorgeous as she was, he sensed there was a lot going on behind those forget-me-not eyes. Not all of it good, either. "I was just giving you an example of when being stubborn is bad. Which you asked me for, by the way."

"Fair enough." A few moments later, she said, "For the record, I'd only go into a burning building to save people or puppies."

"How 'bout kittens?" he teased, getting a laugh for his trouble.

"Okay, anything breathing. Does that cover it for you?"

"Sure."

Their trip back to Toyland went a lot quicker than the walk out, and he was sorry to see it end. Now that she'd opened up a little, he wished he could have a few more minutes to talk to her. Then again, he cautioned himself as they offloaded their goodies, that could only lead to trouble. He wasn't a superficial guy, but experience had taught him to be extremely cautious about relationships. Getting too attached set you up for a lot of heartache when things didn't work out. It was safer to keep some distance in case things went south.

Because, from what he'd seen so far, they always did. It was just a question of how long it took and how much it hurt when you hit bottom.

Chapter Two

The cookies were no problem, but Lauren quickly realized the sandwich platter would never fit in the small fridge Julia kept in her office for cold drinks.

"Come on." Angling her helper toward the door marked Private, she headed up to Julia's apartment. "We'll put them in the kitchen upstairs."

When she was about halfway up, a highbrow English accent called out, "Brevity is the soul of wit!"

Giggling, she looked back at Ben. "You probably know Shakespeare."

"Oh, yeah," he replied with a chuckle. "The Bard and me, we go way back. I thought Julia was just bird-sitting, though. Is she keeping him for good?"

"His owner, Liam, will be at the wedding,"

Lauren explained as they continued up. "He's an interpreter, and his last assignment will be over then. After that, they're on their way back to Wales."

When they reached the top, a huge blue-and-yellow macaw nodded at them with what struck Lauren as a regal bow. "Greetings, fair maiden." Eyeing Ben, he skidded to the side of his perch and adopted a more modern pose. "Wassup, dude?"

Ben laughed, and she shook her head at him. "You taught him that, didn't you?"

"Yeah. You can only take so much classic literature."

"Between that and the kids teaching him nursery rhymes, it'll take Liam months to re-train him."

"Who knows," Ben said as they went into the galley kitchen at the back of Julia's apartment. "Maybe he'll appreciate some variety."

"I'd imagine he'll be glad to be home for a while," she said while she opened the fridge and moved things around to make room for the platter. "He's been going from one post to another for most of the last year."

"Kinda cool, being able to travel around like that," Ben commented with more than a hint of envy. "You get sick of one place, you just pack up and check out somewhere else."

Lauren had done that, leaving a quiet Philadelphia neighborhood for the sparkling Big Apple she'd always longed to explore. In the end, she'd discovered it wasn't *where* you were that mattered. It was *who* you were with. "It's not as fun as it sounds. If you're not with the right person, you could be living in a castle, and it's still awful."

As he handed over the sandwiches, Ben frowned. "You sound like someone who has some personal experience with castles."

And princes, Lauren added silently. The problem was, the ones she kissed kept turning into frogs, instead of the other way around. She used to believe there was someone for everyone, but lately she couldn't help wondering if that philosophy needed some fine-tuning. "Let's just say I've done my time in the tower and I'm not in a hurry to go back."

Her attempt at humor had the effect she was after, and he grinned. "Rapunzel. Ever since she saw the movie, my niece Allie is crazy about that story. She always says if that was her, she'd never have let them put her up there in the first place."

"Good for her," Lauren approved. "I wish I'd thought of that."

He gave her an encouraging smile. "We all

make mistakes, Lauren. It's what we do afterward that really counts."

The simple wisdom in his words touched her deeply. In the brief time she'd known him, she'd gotten more warmth and understanding from him than she had in a year with Jeremy. If only she'd known more guys like Ben, she might have caught on to Jeremy's scheme in time to save herself a lot of heartache.

Shoving the past into the back of her mind for now, she closed the fridge and smiled up at Ben. "Thanks for your help. I should get back down there to help Julia set up for the party."

He cocked his head like he'd just heard something unusual. "You don't sound thrilled with that."

"Well," she hedged then decided she might as well come clean. "I'm not used to kids, so I'm not sure what to expect."

"You'll do fine," he assured her with a confidence she wished she could tap into. "Kids love making Easter eggs and eating snacks, so there's not much for you to do except make sure they don't dye their friend's hair purple or something."

"You almost make it sound like fun," she said as they went back through the apartment.

"It is if you let it be. Like most things, if you let it feel like a chore, then it's no fun at all."

Pausing beside Julia's enormous dollhouse, he made a face. "Like this beast. Nick wanted it to be a Christmas Eve surprise, so he shanghaied me to put it together and bring it up here while Julia was gone. Not my favorite kinda job, but since it was for her, I went along."

"She absolutely adores it," Lauren told him sincerely. "It was really nice of you to help out."

"Well, I couldn't leave Nick to do it himself. He doesn't know a screwdriver from an impact wrench."

Neither did Lauren, but she kept that to herself as they went back downstairs. Closing the door behind them, she looked up into those bright blue eyes as they crinkled in a smile. For her, she realized. He was trying to build up her confidence, to drive away some of the uncertainty that had dogged her every step since leaving New York. Who did that for a stranger? she wondered. She'd given him no encouragement whatsoever, and yet he'd still been so kind to her, she couldn't help wanting to spend more time with him.

Bad idea. Very, very bad.

"Thanks for the advice about the kids," she said politely. "Have a good day."

"You, too, princess."

With that, he sent Julia a quick wave and

headed for the door. Lauren tried not to stare after him, really she did. But she couldn't help herself, and was mortified to realize she was still watching him when Julia glided up next to her and bumped her shoulder.

"Earth to Lauren."

"Hmm?" Her old friend laughed, and Lauren realized she'd been set up by a pro. Glaring over, she asked, "What were you thinking, tossing us together that way?"

"That you need to meet a nice guy who would treat you the way you deserve." Nodding at the view outside the front window, she added, "I think Ben fits the bill nicely, don't you?"

She wanted to deny it, but that would be transparently stupid, so she shrugged. "Maybe."

"Oh, come on! There's not a single woman within a hundred miles who wouldn't kill for the kind of attention you've gotten from him today."

"I'm sure," Lauren replied primly. "He looks like the cheerleader type."

"You were a cheerleader," Julia pointed out, blue eyes twinkling merrily. "I think you two look fabulous together, but there's more to it than that. He's a real sweetheart, and you could use some of that in your life. You don't have to marry him or anything. I was just hoping you two might hit it off and enjoy spending some time together while you're here."

"But when you get back from your honeymoon, I'm leaving," Lauren reminded her.

Julia responded with a cryptic smile. "We'll see. I came for a two-week vacation and realized this is where I was meant to be. Maybe you'll do the same."

"I'm not sure where I belong, but it's certainly not here."

"We'll see," her friend repeated, going to the door when the bells above it announced the first of their egg-coloring guests.

Lauren was a little baffled by her debate with Julia, but one thing was certain. She had no intention of getting attached to this tiny fishing village or the very appealing Ben Thomas. She'd left behind the life she'd once been convinced she wanted, and she simply didn't have the heart to open herself up for any more disappointment.

As she crossed into the crafts section of Toyland, she saw there were about ten kids of various ages scattered around while a handful of parents clustered near the coffee and Danishes Julia had set up for them. The boss was her usual brilliant self, chatting up parents and kids with equal enthusiasm. At a loss for what to do, Lauren took a few minutes to assess the situation before jumping in.

To her surprise, a little girl in a pink T-shirt and denim capris approached her. Giving Lauren a quick once-over, she offered up an adorable gap-toothed grin. "You look like you need a friend."

If this had been an adult, the forthright manner would have startled Lauren. Since she towered over her greeter, though, it was just cute. Hunkering down, she offered her hand. "You can never have too many friends. My name's Lauren."

With a firm shake, the girl said, "I'm Hannah Martin. Julia's going to be my aunt soon."

Julia gushed about the Martin family, so Lauren felt as if she knew them already. "I hear you're going to be the flower girl at their wedding. Are you excited?"

"Very. It's an important job, and I have to do it right. Mommy and Julia took me shopping in Portland to buy me a special dress and fancy white shoes. They're beautiful," she added with a dreamy sigh.

Lauren smiled as her memory flipped back to her own childhood, playing princesses with her sisters. What little girl didn't like dressing up for make-believe? "Are you carrying a basket or a bouquet?"

"Both," Hannah informed her proudly. "I have to toss rose petals out of the basket, but I get to hold on to my flowers. I'm gonna keep them *for-ever*."

"Forever, huh? How long is that?"

Hannah squinted her eyes, scrunching her nose in concentration. "Well, I'm five now, but some people live to be a hundred. Maybe when I'm in kindergarten I can figure it out."

"No doubt," Lauren agreed with a laugh. "When you do, let me know."

"Okay."

Another girl at the front door squealed her name, and Hannah skipped off to meet her. When Julia had first suggested she help out at Toyland, Lauren hadn't been sure about the idea. It wasn't that she disliked children, she mused while she circled the table arranging chairs and supplies for Easter eggs and the coloring contest. She just didn't have any experience with anything other than rocking her infant nephew.

Apparently, Hannah noticed her apprehension and went out of her way to make Lauren feel welcome. Their lighthearted exchange was a success, and she was warming up to the idea of working here, at least for a while. Hopefully, this was the beginning of good things to come.

"All right, everyone!" Julia announced. "Welcome to Toyland's very first Easter Egg-stravaganza."

The parents laughed, but most of the kids looked blankly at each other. Hannah caught on first, and she burst out laughing. "I get it— eggs. That's funny."

Julia rewarded her with a bright smile and a slight bow. "We've got eggs to color and an art contest to judge. Are you ready to get started?"

They all cheered, and Lauren wisely stepped back while they raced toward the paper-covered tables.

After that, the day flew by in a blur of boiled eggs, crayons, trips to the bathroom and tons of cookies. By her estimate, the kids ranged in age from three to nine, and their artistic ability varied widely. Some preferred pastels, others left their eggs in the dye to take on rich, jewel tones.

Crouching down beside one very intent boy later that afternoon, Lauren caught his name from the tag on his shirt. "How's it going, Adam?"

"Fine." Shoving wire-rimmed glasses up on his pug nose, he dipped his egg into a fresh color. "Black is all the colors mixed together, so I'm trying to make a black egg."

Lauren was stunned by the scientific spin to what she'd always considered a childish task. "Really? I didn't know that."

He nodded earnestly. "It was on the science show yesterday. I thought it was cool."

"So do I." Smiling, she stood to move around the table. "Let me know how it turns out."

"Will do."

He sounded so grown-up, she had to ask, "How old are you?"

"Seven, but Mom says I'm going on thirty. I'm not sure why, but that's what she says."

Glancing back, Lauren noticed one of the moms watching them with curiosity. Grinning at her, Lauren said, "Moms are pretty smart, so she must be right."

The woman responded with an approving smile of her own, and Adam nodded. "She usually is. Except when it comes to broccoli. I really hate broccoli."

Lauren laughed for about the tenth time in an hour, and it felt amazing. Her life had lurched down a dark, somber road, and it was wonderful to feel some of the clouds lifting from over her head.

No doubt about it—this was the best day she'd had in a long, long time.

* * *

Tuesday morning, Ben stood at the kitchen counter wolfing down a bowl of cereal. He had a packed schedule of jobs today, and he checked the microwave clock to see it was almost seven. Slurping down the last of his milk, he quickly rinsed his dishes and put them in the dishwasher. His coffee wasn't quite done dripping, but he interrupted the cycle and grabbed the stainless-steel travel mug on his way out the door.

Outside, he jumped in his truck and headed to the other side of town. When he pulled in at his father's place, it was quiet as a tomb. It was time to be up getting ready for work, so he interpreted the lack of movement as a bad sign. Ben used his key to let himself in, bracing himself for what he knew he'd find.

Sprawled out on the living room sofa, his father was sound asleep, cradling an old wedding picture in his arms. Empty whiskey bottles were toppled on the coffee table, where Ben found a very official-looking gray envelope and duplicate sets of legal papers stapled into covers. A quick glance showed him they were final divorce papers, and a flash of anger shot through him.

Mom had been gone nearly a year now, but he still couldn't understand how thirty-five years of marriage ended up printed out in triplicate and neatly bound for filing. It was enough to make even the most optimistic soul doubt the possibility of happily ever after.

His stomach turned at the realization that his disconnected family would never be whole again. He could only imagine what yesterday's mail delivery had done to his brokenhearted father. How could his own wife hurt him this way? Like any family, they had their problems, but Ben couldn't recall anything truly awful. When had things gotten so bad that his mother had decided her only option was to run away?

He'd asked himself those questions a million times. Since he was no closer to an answer now than before, he focused on what he could do something about. Tucking the papers in their envelope, he shoved them in a nearby drawer to get them out of sight. Then he cleared a spot on the table and sat facing his father.

"Dad?" When he got no response, he repeated it a little louder. There was a shudder, followed by a general ripple of movement. "Dad, it's Ben. Wake up."

Squinting against the weak sunlight, he focused bleary eyes on Ben. "Morning."

It was a start. The lecture he'd been set to give went straight out of his head, and he went with sympathy. "I see you had a bad night. Why didn't you call me?"

"I—" He seemed to realize he was still holding the picture, and he set it on the table before pulling himself into a sitting position. "I wanted some time alone."

"With your old friends." Ben nodded at the collection of empties and was pleased to see his father grimace.

"I bought 'em in Oakbridge and came straight back here. I passed half a dozen bars on my way, but I didn't stop. I was sober when I was driving, and that's the truth."

The vow got Ben's attention, and he changed tracks. "I believe you, but this has been going on long enough, and I'm thinking maybe it's time you talk to someone about it. You're not doing so well on your own."

He chewed on that for a minute then frowned. "You're probably right, but shrinks cost money I don't have."

"Pastor McHenry is real easy to talk to. You could go see him." When that got him nowhere, Ben made one more desperate attempt. "You've always enjoyed going to church, but you haven't been there since Christmas Eve. Why don't we go together on Sunday? I'll even take you to brunch at the Albatross afterward."

"I'll think about it." Standing, he added, "Meantime, I'll go get ready for work."

He was more than a little unsteady, and Ben almost told him to take the day off. The trouble was, he feared that with nothing to occupy his time, Dad would stare at that old picture and drink himself back into oblivion.

So, despite his misgivings, he got to his feet and forced optimism into his tone. "Sounds good. I'll see you at the lighthouse."

"Yes, you will." The fog lifted from his eyes, and he gave Ben the bright, genuine smile he hadn't seen in far too long. "I haven't been much of a father lately, but I'm real proud of you, how responsible you are. You know that, don't you?"

Ben's heart swelled with pride, and he swallowed around the lump that had unexpectedly appeared in his throat. *This* was his father, the honest small-town boy who'd married his high school sweetheart and built a business with equal parts sweat and integrity. He'd been stumbling a lot lately, but with some help, Ben believed he could recover. "Yeah, Dad. I know."

"Good." Patting Ben's arm, he shuffled back through the hallway that led to the bathroom.

Taking a few moments to get his emotions back under wraps, Ben dialed the lighthouse's number. Mavis wasn't as spry as she used to be, so he waited patiently for her to answer. "If you're gonna be late, I don't wanna hear it. I got four buckets overflowing in my sitting room."

"Just wanted to let you know we're running a little late this morning. I'll come out and prep and Dad'll join up with me later."

"That don't sound good." Suddenly, the gruffness was gone, and in a gentler tone she said, "I saw him yesterday afternoon, and he looked like he got run over by a backhoe. Is he all right?"

Out of respect for his father's dignity, Ben hesitated. Then again, Mavis had been a close friend of the Thomases for more than forty years. If anyone would understand what was going on, it would be her. "More or less. The divorce papers came from Mom's lawyer yesterday, and he didn't take it well."

"That poor man," she clucked in sympathy. "Are you sure he should be working?"

"I think it's the best thing for him. I'll give him some easy stuff to do to keep him busy, and anything tricky I'll handle myself. You have my word your ceiling will be good as new when we're done."

"Never doubted that. I'll have the coffee ready when you get here."

With that, she hung up, and he shut off his phone. He could hear the shower running, so he figured it was okay for him to go. On his way out, he made a detour to take care of whatever had started smelling up the house since he was here last. He grabbed a large bag from under the sink and did a quick circuit of the living room and kitchen, dropping in things that should have been tossed out a while ago.

He was officially behind schedule, but he took a couple of minutes to get the coffee-maker going. Taking out a loaf of bread and the butter, he left them next to the toaster as a not-so-subtle reminder for Dad to have something to eat before leaving. A glance around showed him he hadn't missed anything, and he left the trash in the outside bin on his way back to his truck. Any psychiatrist worth their salt would probably tell him he was making a huge mistake, cleaning up after a grown man who was perfectly capable of doing it himself.

The problem was, Ben couldn't bring himself to leave things the way he'd found them. It was too depressing.

Early-morning sunshine woke Lauren the following day even before her alarm went off. After a long, fun day, she'd conked out around eight-thirty and hadn't moved until just now. Julia's guest room was in the front of the apartment, with a wide window that looked east, out toward the harbor. When she got up to take a peek outside, she saw the glass was a little frosty, but the sun was rapidly turning Jack Frost's work into streams of water that glinted as they trickled down the window.

Edging the window open, she clearly heard some very optimistic birds in the trees out front, and noticed two that kept flying back and forth to the eaves under the sloping roof. Farther afield, she registered the sounds of people starting their days in the shops along Main Street. One voice called out a cheerful greeting and was met with a grumpier response as a truck started up and drove away.

Suddenly, Lauren wasn't satisfied with observing. She wanted to be out in that crisp New England morning, drinking in the sights and sounds of this place that had offered her a safe haven from the demons haunting her former life. Pulling on jeans and the hand-knit fisherman's sweater she'd bought her first day in town, she jammed on her sneakers and crept down the short hallway to avoid waking Julia. Fortunately, the usually talkative Shakespeare was in his little canvas tent, and she made it downstairs with just a quiet squeak on the old steps.

Outside, she paused on the sidewalk in front of Toyland and took in a deep breath. Chilly and clear as a bell, the air was scented with coffee and spices wafting up from the bakery. It wasn't even seven yet, so she had plenty of time for a walking breakfast. Drawn in by the delicious smell, she headed over to find out what was on the menu at Holiday Harbor Sweets this morning.

Within a few minutes, she was holding a large cup of hazelnut coffee and a bear claw still warm from the oven, dripping with the yummiest icing she'd ever tasted. Deciding she'd already seen all there was of the small downtown, she set out in the other direction, toward the harbor, to check out what was going on down there.

Accustomed to the hectic pace of a large city, she thoroughly enjoyed the opportunity to wander around at a more leisurely clip. She didn't want to get in the way of the crews prepping their boats, but she stood at the top of the large gangway, watching and listening. While the men hollered back and forth, rigging squeaked and clanged, all of it underscored by the calls of circling gulls overhead. It was as if they were staking out their territory, reminding the fishermen they'd be waiting for their share when the boats returned later in the day.

Here, the air was heavier, dosed with salt and the smell of diesel engines. A steady line of boats headed out to sea, in an orderly floating parade that suggested they did it this way every single day. A metallic clang caught her attention, and Lauren looked out to find the source of the noise. Buoys bobbed in the water, marking the path into the busy wharf. Beyond them, rising up out of the mist, was Last Chance Lighthouse, its slowly rotating beacon cutting a path through the fog.

It didn't look too far away, Lauren decided, backtracking up the ramp to continue her stroll. After hearing Ben's nutshell version of its history, she wouldn't mind seeing it up close. The two-lane blacktop road leading out there needed some work, but it was in prime condition compared to the dirt lane that wound in toward the tower and the small house attached to it.

From here, the activity of the wharf was drowned out by the sound of waves crashing on the rocks that formed the rugged coastline. Drawn in by the awesome power of the ocean, Lauren carefully picked her way down a footpath of sorts that led to the narrow beach. Once she was back on solid ground, she stared out at the water, amazed by the sheer force driving the morning tide toward the shore.

While she finished her breakfast, the salty wind continually blew through her hair, and more than once she almost lost her balance when a strong gust hit her full on. Closing her eyes, she felt the natural currents of wind and water swirling around her and could almost imagine them blowing her past away.

"Not a good idea being down here this time of day." At the sound of Ben's voice, she opened her eyes to find him standing beside her. "Low tide's better for exploring the shoreline."

A little rattled by her instinctive response to the sea, Lauren did her best to laugh it off. "You're right. It's so beautiful, I guess I got carried away."

His laugh was lost in a sudden gush of noise, but his wide grin came through loud and clear. "Didn't really take you for a nature lover. You have any other surprises you're hiding?"

Through harsh experience, she'd learned to be wary of handsome men with disarming grins. Somehow, this one was different. The instincts she'd kept under wraps for the past few months began rustling, assuring her Ben was someone to be trusted. If not with her heart, then at least with her friendship. Offering him a genuine smile, she teased, "A lady never tells."

"Right."

As the rising sun glinted off the incoming water, for the first time she noticed it swirling into depressions along the rocky cliffs. "Are those caves down there?"

"Yeah, but most of 'em flood at high tide, so it's best to steer clear unless you're with someone who knows which ones are safe."

He added a knowing look, and she had to laugh. "So you're a mind reader, too?"

"Something like that. I'm headed inside to chat with Mavis about her sitting-room ceiling. Wanna meet her?"

Lauren nearly declined, then changed her mind. It was still early, and she had plenty of time before Toyland opened at ten. What harm could it do? "The woman who makes the killer gingerbread? Absolutely."

Ben held out one of those very capable hands for her, and Lauren's heart beat as fast as a hummingbird's wings. She recognized he was only being considerate, offering to steady her on the uneven ground, but being within arm's reach of him went completely against the polite-but-distant policy she'd adopted for men in general. Reaching for a nice way to refuse the gentlemanly gesture, she wiped her hands on her jeans. "I'm all sticky, but thanks."

Confusion flashed in his eyes but quickly evaporated as he shrugged and trudged up the hill beside her. When they reached the tower's gravelly yard, the bright red front door opened. An older woman dressed in baggy slacks and a moth-eaten sweater stepped out holding a leash in her hand. The animal at the other end of it made Lauren stop dead in her tracks. "What in the world is that?"

"That's Reggie," Ben explained as they continued up the pathway. "He's a pot-bellied pig."

The woman lived alone in a lighthouse on the edge of the sea, made gingerbread and kept a pig for a pet. Lauren had seen some odd things since arriving in Holiday Harbor, but this one definitely took the cake.

"Mavis Freeman," Ben began, "this is Lauren Foster. She's gonna be helping Julia out at Toyland."

Squinting at Lauren, Mavis studied her intently while Reggie snuffled around her sneakers. It was a strange way to greet someone, but Lauren did her best to look and sound friendly. "Good morning, Ms. Freeman. You have a beautiful home."

That got her a furious glare. "It's *Mrs*. Freeman. I don't truck with all that modern feminist nonsense."

"Mavis is the keeper's widow," Ben said almost reverently. Lauren would have found that description slightly insulting, but Mavis beamed at him as if he'd proclaimed her queen.

"That's right. I don't know where you're from, missy, but there's still folks around who do things the old-fashioned way."

"Actually, I'm from Philadelphia," Lauren replied as pleasantly as she could manage. Instinct warned her that her stint in New York was best left out of this conversation. "With all that history around us, we like doing things the old-fashioned way, too."

Some of the disapproval left their hostess's expression, and she gave a short nod. "All right, then."

Uncertain if she'd passed muster with the brusque keeper or not, Lauren opted to shift her attention to Reggie. After circling her a few times, he politely sat in front of her. Looking up at Lauren with what could only be described as a smile, he wagged his bristly tail for all he was worth. Grateful for the distraction, she knelt down and scratched behind his floppy ears. "You're a real cutie. How'd you end up here?"

Apparently, to get on Mavis's good side, all

you had to do was be kind to her unusual pet. Her lined face cracking into a smile, she explained, "We're a pair, me and Reggie. A little tough on the eyes, but for the right kinda folks, we got good hearts. Don't we, boy?"

He grunted his agreement, and Lauren couldn't help laughing as she stood. "That's awesome. It's a pleasure to meet you both."

Mavis took the hand she offered, and Lauren felt as if she'd made a huge leap toward fitting into her temporary home. Glancing over at Ben, she registered the concern on his face and frowned. "Is something wrong?"

"Nope, but my dad'll be here soon, so I'd best get to work inside."

He turned to go, but Mavis called him back. "Where's your manners gone to? The girl needs a ride back to town."

"Oh, I'm fine," Lauren assured her. "I walked out here, and it's not any farther going back."

Crossing her arms in obvious disapproval, the woman didn't say anything but pinned Ben with a stern, unyielding look. Shaking his head, he grinned at Lauren. "Okay, then. Guess I'm driving you back to Toyland."

"It's really not—"

"Just be quiet and go along," he murmured,

motioning her toward his truck. "It's not a big deal."

Figuring he knew best, she said goodbye to Mavis and Reggie and climbed into the passenger seat. As they started back, she said, "What was that all about?"

"Nothing. It's just easier to go along when she gets stubborn like that."

A few seconds later, she caught on and started laughing. "Let me guess. When you were a kid, she scared you half to death."

The sideways glance he slid her told her she'd hit that one dead-on. "Fine, she did. But to be fair, she scared everyone under the age of ten. Then when her husband died a few years ago—" he shrugged "—I think she got lonely, so she started being a little nicer. She and Dad are old friends, so we help out with the lighthouse and the residence when she needs something repaired. Or someone to have coffee with."

"You're good to her, so she's good to you."

"Yeah, I guess."

Touched by the sweet, simple story, Lauren sighed. "That's how it's supposed to be. If everyone did that, the world would be a much better place."

As they pulled onto Main Street, Ben added, "That's why they call it the Golden Rule."

"I guess."

To Lauren, it sounded too good to be true, but she recognized that was her ingrained skepticism talking. She didn't used to be that way, she lamented. What had happened to the girl who'd believed there was good in everyone? Sadly, she knew the answer, but she didn't want to spoil such a beautiful, sunny morning with dark thoughts.

Outside Toyland, Ben pulled to a stop and got out to open her door. Climbing down, she stood inside the open door, much closer to him than she'd intended. Oddly enough, the anxiety she'd felt on the beach earlier was much less intense, and the smile she gave him was only slightly forced. Maybe she was finally getting a little of her old confidence back. She wasn't rock solid yet, but being within Ben's reach was a good first step.

Squinting against the rising sun, she said, "Thanks for the ride. Be sure to tell Mavis you delivered me in one piece."

"Will do. Have a good day."

"You, too."

That got her another, even brighter grin than she'd yet seen from him. He seemed to have an endless collection of them, each one more endearing than the last. As he got back in and drove away, he waved through the back window, and like a sentimental damsel in an old movie, she caught herself waving back. All she was missing was the lacy handkerchief, she groused as she unlocked the door to Toyland.

But as she made her way upstairs, she allowed herself a little smile. For the first time in ages, she'd had a couple of uninterrupted hours to herself, and they were wonderful. What was so special about them? she wondered while she started the coffeemaker in the kitchen. On her way into the bathroom, she came to the conclusion that nothing extraordinary had happened except that she'd enjoyed doing absolutely nothing but breathe.

Maybe, she thought with a little grin at her reflection, that was the whole point.

Chapter Three

"I think this should do it, Mavis," Ben announced, tapping the supply list he'd made. "That section of roof needs to be replaced, then we can fix the ceiling. I'll get everything we need, and we'll be back tomorrow to get started."

She accepted his comment with her characteristic nod. "There's rain coming this weekend, you know."

"We won't be totally done by then, but we'll make sure it's buttoned up against the weather, don't you worry. Right, Dad?"

"Right."

Ben had made several clumsy attempts to include his father in the discussion with their client, as much to keep him engaged as to be polite. Quiet but steady, Dad was obviously doing his best to stay focused, but Ben had a sneaking suspicion if he left him alone for five minutes, he'd be asleep on his feet.

"I really should get into Landry's Books and finish installing that cabinet," Ben commented, uneasy about leaving his father alone.

As if sensing his discomfort, Mavis patted his shoulder in an unexpectedly motherly gesture and nudged him toward the door. "You go on. Me and Craig'll have some lunch and a nice long chat."

The prospect of food perked Dad up considerably, and he gave her a fond smile. "I'd like that very much. Thank you."

Pleased by the upturn his worrisome morning had taken, Ben teased, "You sure I can leave you two kids alone out here?"

"Oh, you," Mavis clucked, the faint blush on her cheeks telling him he'd managed to flatter the crustiest woman in town. "Get outta here before I put you to work in my vegetable garden."

Ben made a show of bolting for the exit, letting the outer door slam behind him. As he strolled out to his truck, he heard laughter inside and congratulated himself on successfully navigating what could have been an awkward situation. His father needed someone to talk to, a friend who'd listen to his problems without judging. Since Ben hadn't gotten anywhere with him, he was grateful for any help Mavis could give.

On his way into town, he finally had a chance to mull over his odd discussion with Lauren that morning. Her baffling comments made it painfully obvious that she'd been through something awful recently, and his gut was almost certain that was why she'd unexpectedly landed in his hometown. What was she hiding? he wondered.

They'd just met, so it had nothing to do with him, which meant it was strictly none of his business. Even if by some stretch of the imagination he could do something about it, he wasn't keen on adding Julia's troubled friend to his already lengthy list of responsibilities. Still, he couldn't help wishing there was something he could do to help her.

When Ben got to Landry's Books, the owner Amelia Landry, met him at the door with a worried frown. "What's wrong?"

"Nothing, just had to finish up something out at the lighthouse before I came here."

Eyes narrowing, she gave him the Mom look. "If you don't want to tell me, fine, but I know something's up with you. Cooper gets that same look on his face when he's chewing on something."

As a single mother, she'd more or less

adopted her son's friends as her own. Even though they were all adults now, she still watched over them. With his own mother completely out of the picture, Ben appreciated Amelia now more than ever.

But he'd never share his suspicions about Lauren with anyone, so he just grinned. "It's really nothing, but thanks. Now, the sooner I get back to work on those cabinets, the sooner I'll be out of your hair."

While he opened his toolbox, Amelia made a good show of fussing over a display of Easter figurines and doodads set out for the holiday. The original formation looked fine to him, so he guessed that she was stalling, trying to frame whatever it was she had to say.

"I saw you in town with Julia's friend yesterday," she began. "She's quite an eyeful."

Setting a hinge in place, he chuckled. "Yup, she's real pretty." Actually, she was a stunner straight out of some old Hollywood movie, but admitting that would open him up for all kinds of probing questions, so he kept that detail to himself.

"What's her name?"

Ben knew perfectly well the local gossip mill had churned out that bit of information long before Lauren even arrived in town. Because he liked Amelia, he played along. "Lauren Foster."

"What a lovely name. Is she nice?"

That wasn't the right term, but Ben was surprised to find he couldn't come up with a one-word description of her. She was clearly bright and talented, but she had a darkness about her that struck him as completely out of place. That contradiction intrigued him more than it should, and to get back on track, he simply said, "Yeah, she's nice."

"I hear Julia adores her," Amelia went on, using a feather duster on a collection of pint-size forest gnomes. "She's been worried about her, though. It seems Lauren's gotten herself tangled up with someone who's not very good for her."

"I'm pretty sure they broke up," Ben blurted without thinking. Embarrassed to be gossiping, he focused on the hinge to conceal his sudden discomfort.

"Really? Well, that's a whole new ball game then, isn't it?"

Glancing up, Ben caught Amelia eyeing him, then laughed when she abruptly turned her attention to a nearby shelf that was already perfectly arranged. "And you think I should step up to the plate, is that it?"

"I'm just saying there's more to this life than

work and more work. When's the last time you had a date?"

"Church social last month."

"You sat with the pastor and his family then ended up washing dishes till midnight. That's not the kind of socializing a young man needs, and you know it." Setting the duster aside, she hunkered down beside him. "Ben, your mom and I were friends all through school, but what she's done to all of you is just plain wrong. When things get tough, you don't turn your back on the people who need you."

Ben had never discussed the breakup of his family with anyone, and it still made him sick to think about it. After an honorable discharge from the military, his older brother, Eric, was roaming around New England, working odd jobs and still trying to find his place. Three years ago, his sister, Casey had moved to Detroit with her husband and young children. That left Ben alone to manage their father's troubling downhill slide.

Amelia's honest sympathy had nudged a crack into his characteristic self-control, and he heard himself say, "The divorce is final now. Dad's taking it pretty hard."

"Of course he is. Divorces are awful, even when you both agree it's the best thing for everyone."

Ben didn't have a response for that, so he just nodded. Having gone through it herself when Cooper was young, he figured she knew what she was talking about.

Standing, she folded her arms and looked down at him. "What you need is to have some fun. This girl won't be in town forever, so you should ask her out sooner rather than later."

"What makes you think I even want to?" She tipped her head in a chiding gesture, and he laughed. "Okay, maybe I was tempted for about five seconds, but she's one of those uptown girls who needs a room-sized closet to hold all her shoes. Not exactly my type."

"I'm not saying marry her," she argued, "I'm saying go to a movie or something. You only live once, and you should make sure you grab a little fun along the way."

Maybe she was right, he thought. Lauren had snared his attention the moment he met her, and he was more than a little curious about what made her tick. She'd left her ex behind in New York, so there was no reason for Ben to keep his distance. Amelia's suggestion was worth thinking about, anyway. Since Lauren was new in town, she didn't know anyone but Julia, who was busy with her wedding. He could invite Lauren over for a good meal and some friendly conversation, no strings attached. Where was the harm in that?

Of course, if he shared his train of thought with Amelia, he'd never hear the end of it. Instead, he fended off her repeated attempts at a fix-up until he finished with her cabinets. The day had gotten away from him, so by the time Ben filled his supply list and checked in with Thomas and Sons other ongoing jobs, it was eight o'clock when he got home.

Too tired for anything beyond a glass of water, he kicked off his boots and fell into bed. Out of habit, he checked his voice mail and saw he had a message from an old buddy of his who now lived in Boston. Wondering what might be up, he played the recording.

"Hey, man, it's Davy. Just took on a restoration job in Concord and could really use a top-notch guy like you. The project starts June 1, so you can crash with me till you find a place down here. Call me and I'll give you the deets. Later."

Intrigued, Ben started to call, but paused with his thumb hovering over the return button. He and Davy both loved old houses, and had spent summers helping to refurbish many of the eighteenth-and nineteenth-century homes in and around Holiday Harbor. While he accepted the general contracting work he was doing now, nothing made Ben happier than to restore an old building to its former glory. That was why he'd taken on the challenging job at Toyland. It had required a ton of research and painstaking work, but every time he walked in there, he felt proud to be part of bringing the neglected old storefront back to life.

But right now, Thomas and Sons needed him more than Davy did. Eric might be home next week, or he might never come back. Ben had no way of knowing, but he couldn't bring himself to abandon his father. Even if it was the opportunity of a lifetime.

Sighing, he saved the message and plugged his phone in to charge. All he had to do was close his eyes and he was sound asleep.

It didn't last. When his phone lit up and started ringing, he groaned in protest, then rolled over and pulled the pillow over his head. Whoever it was could get a life and leave him a message. If he didn't get some sleep, he wouldn't make it through tomorrow, much less the rest of the week. The phone went silent, but not for long. When it started up again, he realized it must be important and flopped onto his back to check the caller ID.

Eric. His big brother was a night owl, but he knew good and well Ben wasn't. Something was wrong, and he thumbed the answer function. "Yeah?"

"Tell me Dad's with you."

The blood in Ben's veins froze in place, and he cautioned himself not to overreact. Taking a deep breath, he said, "He's not. Why?"

"We were supposed to meet here in Rockland for dinner, but he never showed. I called his cell, but it went right to voice mail. Same with the house phone."

"He and Mavis had lunch today," Ben suggested. "Maybe he's still out at the lighthouse."

"That's the first place I called."

Rubbing his gritty eyes with one hand, he asked, "Did you try the bars in Oakbridge?"

"Yeah, but nobody remembers seeing him. I'm getting worried."

That was an understatement, Ben knew. Having served ten years as an Army Ranger, not much rattled his big brother. If Eric admitted to being concerned about something, the average person would be downright hysterical. "It's not like him to disappear like this. Where could he be?"

"You don't think—"

He stopped abruptly, and a feeling of dread crept up Ben's spine. "Think what?"

"That he did something, y'know, desperate?"

Ben's heart thudded to a stop. It wasn't unheard of for people to go up to Schooner Point and fling themselves from the high rocky cliff into the ocean. He should have gone by the lighthouse that afternoon as he'd planned, to check on Dad as much as the job. But he'd gotten so preoccupied with Lauren and the baffling effect she had on him, it had completely slipped his mind. After their heart-to-heart that morning, Dad might have interpreted Ben's inadvertent absence the wrong way. Ben had to find him and make sure he was safe.

"Thanks for letting me know," Ben said while he retied his boots. "I'll call you when I find him."

"You mean *if*," Eric retorted gloomily.

"I mean *when*," he insisted, refusing to even consider any other possibility. His family might be in pieces, but everyone was safe and sound. Ben was determined to do everything in his power to keep it that way.

"I hope you're right. I'll be up late, so call anytime."

On that slightly more optimistic note, he hung up. Sighing, Ben tilted his head back and sent up a heartfelt prayer. "I know You've got a lot to do, but I could really use Your help down here."

Figuring that sentiment pretty much covered it, he grabbed a spare jacket and jumped into his truck. The fuel gauge hovered just above *E,* and he bit back an exasperated scream while he backtracked to the garage for the gas can he used on job sites. It was half-empty, but he drained it into his tank while he mentally added "stop at gas station" to his list for tomorrow morning.

"Long stinkin' list," he growled as he finally pulled out. "I need an assistant or something."

While it did nothing to solve the problem, complaining to himself vented some of his frustration, so he kept going with it as he made a circuit of all the places in town his father might go. It didn't take long to discover the other Thomas and Sons truck was nowhere to be found. That left him with Schooner Point, which had always been one of Dad's favorite spots. It was where he'd proposed to Ben's mother so many years ago, and that he'd head up there now made a twisted kind of sense to Ben.

The sky was clear as a bell, but the sliver of a moon suspended in the darkness didn't provide much in the way of help. As he approached the isolated ridge north of town, he squinted into the distance, searching for something that would tell him someone was up here.

There. A faint dot of light, out near the edge of the cliff. Ignoring the rough-cut road that wound along the tree line, he headed straight for that pinpoint of light, following it like a beacon on the water. When he finally located it, he was relieved to find it was connected to his father's truck.

Glancing up into the star-filled sky, he smiled. "Thank you."

Was it his imagination, or did a star up there shine a little brighter for just a second? Figuring it was his exhausted brain playing tricks on him, Ben shook off the ridiculous idea and climbed out of his seat. Heading toward the ridge, he put his hands in the front pockets of his jeans to give the appearance of a guy out for a casual nighttime stroll.

When he reached the truck, he saw his dad inside, staring out at miles of starlit ocean. He'd often mentioned bringing Ben's mother here when they were dating, and how they'd stay for hours, admiring the view and talking about their dreams for the future. Tonight, he looked like he was lost in memories of what used to be.

To avoid startling him, Ben tapped lightly on the driver's window. After another tap, his father blinked and looked out at him in surprise. When he rolled down the window, the strains of "Fly Me to the Moon" floated from the cab, and Ben swallowed hard. It was his mother's favorite song.

Keeping things light, he forced a grin. "Hey, there."

Apparently, he was a terrible actor, because he got a frown for his trouble. "Is something wrong?"

"Eric's been waiting in Rockland half the night for you." Leaning his arms on the window frame, he added, "You were supposed to have dinner with him."

Dad leaned his head back against the seat with a groan. "I forgot."

"Mind if I join you?"

He motioned Ben inside, and once he was settled, Ben called his brother. "I found him up at the point. He's fine."

"Good. Give him a good shake for me, wouldya?"

Ben didn't think that would help much, so he suggested, "Why don't you come up this weekend? You can do it yourself."

Despite his gruff demeanor, Ben knew Eric would never lay a hand on anyone in anger. After a moment, his brother chuckled. "I'm already over it. Tell him good-night for me."

Ben hung up then took a breath before facing his dad. "We were worried sick about you. What were you thinking, disappearing like that?"

"I was home, getting cleaned up after work, and when I got out of the shower, I stood there for a minute." Meeting Ben's gaze, his face contorted with pain. "Do you know how quiet an empty house is?"

Lately, Ben hadn't been home enough to experience it for himself, but it didn't take much to imagine how it felt to be alone all the time. "Maybe you should leave the radio or TV on, so there's some noise."

"Noise isn't the same as someone being there," Dad explained sadly. "I lived with my parents till I started fixing up that place for your mother and me to live in when we were married. I've never been alone this long in my life. I'm not good at it."

The optimist in Ben wanted to point out he had two sons and plenty of friends to ease that loneliness, but something stopped him. Nearly sixty, his father wasn't talking about simply having company. He needed a companion to spend his off-hours with. Someone to take out to dinner and a movie, someone who argued with him about what color to paint the living room. Since Ben hadn't managed to find that special person for himself, he didn't think he was in a position to give anyone advice on their personal life.

Still, he was a problem solver by nature, and he couldn't just let his father struggle if there was a way to make him feel better while his heart recovered from the tumble it had taken. "Okay, I get that, but you can't just vanish like you did tonight. If one of us calls, you have to answer your phone."

"I will from now on. I'm sorry."

His apology rang with honest remorse, and Ben decided it was time to shove him back into the life he'd once enjoyed so much. "And we're going to church on Sunday."

"I don't—"

"Then on Monday you're gonna make an appointment with either a therapist or Pastor McHenry. I don't care which, but it's long past time you got some help dealing with all this. And don't try to welsh on it," he added sternly, "'cause I'll be checking up on you."

A hint of his father's old spirit flared in his eyes. "You can't do that. I'm an adult."

"When you start acting like one, I'll quit treating you like a four-year-old."

Dad opened his mouth to retort, then slowly closed it and shook his head. "I guess I deserved that one. This must be tough on you, and I apologize for making things so difficult.

A father's supposed to take care of his son, not the other way around."

Filled with regret, that statement summed up the aggravation Ben had been feeling for weeks now. Hearing it laid out in its simplest terms, he forgave his father on the spot. Resting a hand on his arm, Ben said, "Family supports family, no matter how old we get. I'm willing to go on helping as long as you're trying to help yourself."

That got him a wan smile. "Pray to God but row for shore?"

Ben's granddad had fished the Atlantic until the day he died, and that was one of his favorite sayings. Hearing it now made Ben even more confident that his father could navigate his way through these rough waters and find a safe harbor on the other side. "Absolutely. You're as good a sailor as you ever were. You've just lost your bearings. Once we get you a new compass, you'll be fine."

He chewed on that for a minute then nodded. "I like that idea. It sure beats rowing around in circles." After a minute, he added, "When were you gonna tell me about Dave Klein's offer?"

He stiffened reflexively, angry at his friend for making a bad situation worse. "You know about that?"

"Course I do. He called to ask if it was okay with me. I told him I thought it sounded perfect for you. So why didn't you mention it?"

Ben shrugged, hoping to give the impression the opening wasn't that big a deal. "I'm mulling it over."

"Why? Restoring old places is what you're best at, and you love it. What's to mull?"

He didn't have a reasonable answer to that, so he stalled. Finally, inspiration struck. "I have to finish our current jobs before I consider doing anything else."

"We've got things lined up through the fall, and Davy needs you in June. Stay here through Memorial Day, then you'll be in Boston for the nice weather. The timing couldn't be better."

Actually, Ben amended silently, the timing couldn't be worse. Because his father's approval made it possible for him to accept the job, it would make it that much harder for him to say no. He was dying to spread his wings and experience life outside his tiny hometown, but in his heart he knew staying in Holiday Harbor was the right thing for his family. "Like I said, I'm thinking about it."

"This is a great opportunity for you, son. Don't turn it down because of me."

"I won't." Not entirely, anyway. "If you want some company tonight, you're welcome to come home with me. Just remember I snore," he added with a chuckle to lighten the mood.

"I appreciate the offer, but I'll be fine at my place."

Ben hesitated. He wanted to give his dad the benefit of the doubt, but he wasn't sure it was the smart thing to do. The man had gotten rattled by a quiet house and had basically run away. Could he be trusted to stay by himself?

"I'll be fine," he repeated more forcefully. "Go home and get some sleep. You look like you got run over by an 18-wheeler."

"Thanks a lot." Still, the insult came with a slight grin, which was an improvement over what he'd found when he first climbed into the truck. Opening the door, he paused to look his father directly in the eyes, searching for potential trouble. He didn't find any but still said, "Call me if you get lonely again."

"Won't need to," he replied confidently. "I'm gonna set the TV timer so it'll stay on until I fall asleep."

Pleased that his suggestion had been taken well, Ben said, "Okay, then. Night."

"Night, son. Thanks for coming after me."

He almost answered, "Anytime," then thought better of it. Instead, he patted Dad's shoulder and left the cab. Inside his own truck, he waited until he heard the other engine start up. He was tempted to follow the old truck back into town, then realized that might suggest he didn't trust his father to get himself home.

Swallowing his misgivings, Ben headed back to his place for the second time that night. Something told him tomorrow was going to be another long, challenging day. He'd better get some sleep.

Before Lauren could blink, it was Saturday morning. *Early* Saturday morning. Her first week as the assistant manager of Toyland had been a blur of springtime activities Julia had cooked up to draw children and their parents into the store for some fun—and shopping. Being the last day before Easter, today promised to be a doozy, and Lauren would have welcomed the chance to sleep right up until they unlocked the front door.

"Tell me again why we're doing this now instead of last night," she grumbled while she and Julia got dressed at the crack of dawn.

Handing her a steaming cup of Kona blend, her friend responded with something between a yawn and a laugh. "I heard they tried that once years ago, and raccoons stole every last egg. It was a disaster."

Odd as it was, at least that was a good reason for being up so early, Lauren thought while they made their way to the town square. Several people were already there, doing the yawning-laughing thing while an older woman with pink cheeks and a cheerful smile handed out cartons of colored eggs from a child's red wagon.

"Please keep them in the square," she directed a group dressed in heavy sweaters like Lauren's. "Don't put two eggs in the same spot, and if you run out, come find me. There are plenty more. God bless you all for coming out this morning."

Taking Lauren's arm, Julia led her over to get in line. When they reached the front, the woman's face lit up, and she folded Julia into a warm hug. "They're just beautiful!" she approved, motioning to the impressive inventory of eggs. "Letting the children make the eggs they're hunting for was a wonderful idea."

"I'm so glad you're pleased. Lauren Foster, I'd like you to meet Ann McHenry, our pastor's wife and choir director of the Safe Harbor Church. And soon to be my mother-in-law."

While they shook hands, Ann beamed at Lauren as if they'd known each other forever instead of ten seconds. "It's wonderful to meet you. I have to tell you, my granddaughter Hannah thinks you hung the moon."

This woman projected unabashed warmth, and Lauren's habitual reserve melted in the face of it. "She's pretty great herself. All the kids we had in this week were fantastic, but she's something else."

"That she is," Ann said with a trace of a proud Irish lilt. Winking at Julia, she added, "It's a McHenry trait, you know."

Laughing, Julia hugged her around the shoulders and reached in for two buckets of eggs. Handing one to Lauren, she introduced her to the others as they made their way around the large park, tucking eggs here and there as they went.

By the time they reached the white gazebo, Lauren's head was spinning with new faces and the names that went with them. "I can't believe this many people would get up so early to do this. It's so sweet."

"It's a tradition here, making the most of every holiday." Resting a hand on one of the slender columns, she surveyed the grassy square with a smile. "Their devotion to their history is one of the things I like most about this place."

Out of the corner of her eye, Lauren noticed a familiar dark green pickup pulling in next to the church steps. Ben hopped out and headed in their direction, and Lauren couldn't help admiring his long, confident stride as he moved over the grass. A man on a mission, she realized with a little grin. One of the busiest men she'd ever met, he always seemed to be going somewhere but still made time to help out with things like this. It said a lot about the kind of guy he was.

"Morning, ladies." He greeted them with one of his warm smiles. "Nice day for hunting eggs."

"Ben!" Ann called out, and he turned as she hurried up behind them. "Just the man I've been waiting for. Have you got my Easter lilies?"

"And amaryllis and tulips and some other stuff I can't pronounce," he confirmed with a chuckle. "Perry down at the nursery insisted on throwing in some extra plants. Said the display was a little sparse last year, and he wanted to make sure it was top-notch this time."

She huffed derisively. "Sparse? I hardly think so."

"Hey, don't blame me." Ben lifted his hands in self-defense. "I'm just the messenger. Besides, wait'll you get a look at what he sent you. That might make you feel better."

"We'll just see about that," she snapped, obviously smarting over the thinly veiled insult of her previous decorating. The woman's quick temper surprised Lauren. Wasn't the wife of a pastor supposed to be quietly supportive of her husband and his church, not wrangling with local businessmen? Apparently, Ann McHenry did things her own way, Lauren mused. She liked that.

"Ann," Julia offered in a soothing tone, "I'll take over the eggs so the rest of you can get to work inside."

It took Lauren about half a second to understand she was being included in "the rest of you." Because she couldn't think of a single reason to protest, she decided it was best to go along. She and Ben fell into step behind Ann, who walked a lot faster than her appearance would suggest.

"Irish," he murmured, nodding forward with a fond smile.

"And proud of it," Ann retorted loudly, making it clear she'd heard him just fine.

Laughing quietly, Lauren shook her head. It seemed that everyone she'd met in Holiday Harbor had their quirks, and they didn't bother trying to hide them. They accepted people as they were, and they expected the same in return.

During her time in New York, she'd never felt like she fit in with Jeremy's friends. Talking to him about it had gotten her nowhere—

he just told her to make more of an effort. She'd tried everything she knew to be part of the group, but she'd always felt like an outsider. As she stopped near Ben's truck, a new possibility occurred to her.

Maybe the problem hadn't been with her at all. Maybe it was them, looking down on someone who wasn't from their close-knit society circle. No matter what she did, she couldn't have changed where she'd come from, the middle-class upbringing her parents had given her. Now that she had the benefit of some perspective, Lauren understood that there was nothing she could have done to blend in with people like that.

The realization made her feel better about choosing to leave that world behind, and she gratefully turned her attention to whatever job the brisk pastor's wife had for her.

Ann peeked over the side of his pickup, assessing the plants with a critical eye. Lauren was no expert, but they looked lovely to her, bursting with vivid green leaves and flowers running the gamut from ivory to blush to lavender.

Taking out two potted tulips, Ann laughed. "I have to admit, Perry outdid himself this time. Let's get them inside and watered."

"Yes, ma'am," Ben answered dutifully. She

headed inside, and when Lauren stepped up and held out her arms, he gave her a skeptical look. "We're not gonna do this again, are we?"

"Yes, we are. Load me up or I'll tell Ann you turned down free help."

Sighing, he handed her two tall Easter lilies and grabbed a crate packed with sunny daffodils. "You're mean."

While she knew the comment was meant as a joke, it gave a nice little jolt to her attitude, which up to now had been riding pretty low. Tossing her head in the defiant gesture she'd nearly forgotten, she strolled ahead of him. "You have no idea just how mean I can be."

Hearing him chuckling behind her made her smile, and her mood continued to brighten when she got a look inside the quaint white chapel that had captured her attention her first day in town.

Whitewashed walls led up to what must have been a fifteen-foot ceiling braced by hand-hewn timbers. Age had darkened the wood, giving her the sensation of being on an old ship. There were three stained-glass windows on each side, depicting various scenes of boats, farms and the ocean. Some of them included animals and people dressed in homespun clothes, working the land and reeling in nets of fish.

Humble was the word that came to mind while Lauren strolled through to admire the care that had gone into crafting this church. Even the lectern on the raised platform looked original to the building, and she recalled Julia telling her how much these people valued their history. That reverence was on display in every inch of this immaculately kept space, beautiful in its simplicity.

"Pretty, huh?" Ben asked as he passed by her to set a couple of flowerpots on a windowsill.

"Very." Inhaling the mingled sweet scents of a variety of flowers, she added, "And it's going to smell great besides. What are those?"

"Got me," he replied with a shrug. "I'm a hammer-and-nails kinda guy."

"Hyacinths," Ann called out. "Spread them out a little more, Ben, or they'll be too strong."

"Gotcha." Whistling "Here Comes Peter Cottontail," he took one of the lilies Lauren was holding and switched it for one of the hyacinths. To her knowledge, Lauren had never met a man who still knew that song, and hearing it from such a rugged guy made her smile.

Since he had so many plants in his crate, Lauren gave him a hand spreading the daffodils around before they headed out for more.

As they reloaded and went back in, she asked, "You're pretty laid-back, aren't you?"

"Yup."

She hadn't meant to turn this into an actual conversation, but she heard herself say, "Your life seems pretty hectic to me. How do you manage to be so easygoing?"

Setting the crate on a wooden bench between two windows, he gave her his full attention. "You said you're not really into religion, so you might not like my answer."

"I'll keep an open mind."

After hesitating for a moment, very quietly he said, "I do the best I can with what I get, and I leave the hard stuff up to God."

Eloquent in its simplicity, the philosophy suited the solid, down-to-earth contractor perfectly. Unfortunately, Lauren couldn't get her head around it, and she frowned. "That works for you?"

"Mostly. When it doesn't, I know it's 'cause the timing isn't right for what I want. Eventually, everything ends up the way it's supposed to be. We just have to be patient and trust that He knows what He's doing."

"I guess that's why they call it faith," Lauren commented thoughtfully, glancing around the light, airy space. It seemed ideally suited to their unexpected discussion, and she said,

"It's so inviting now, I can only imagine how it is when it's full of people."

"You don't have to imagine it." When she met his eyes, he gave her a gentle smile. "You could tag along with Julia tomorrow and see for yourself."

It was so tempting, she longed to accept. Instead, she hedged. "I don't know. Easter's an important day, and I'm not sure it's right to be here when I don't worship the rest of the year. I'd feel like a hypocrite."

"Like the sign out front says, everyone's welcome. All you have to do is come inside."

He made it sound so easy, but Lauren still wasn't certain she belonged here. Or anywhere, for that matter. But gazing up into Ben's warm, understanding eyes, she found herself wondering if she'd somehow staggered onto the path her life was meant to follow. It had led her to this delightful little town filled with friendly people who liked her instead of judging her.

Since she'd run out of reasons to say no, she relented with a smile. "I'll think about it."

While she helped finish the decorating, an unfamiliar sensation began circling around her, enveloping her in something she hadn't felt in so long, it took her a while to identify the emotion. Finally, she realized what it was.

Contentment.

Instinct told her it was no coincidence that she'd begun to rediscover her old self after leaving Jeremy. More than that, the positive feeling reinforced her decision with a steely resolve that shocked her. Filled with luxuries most people only dreamed of, the glittering lifestyle he'd offered her had captivated her at first.

In the end, it came with a price higher than she was willing to pay. And she was *never* going back.

Chapter Four

Ben watched with curiosity as determination glinted in Lauren's eyes. It muted the bright blue with something darker, and he made a mental note never to do anything that would earn him such a ferocious glare. He might be bigger than her, but he wasn't too proud to admit that look scared him.

A woman scorned? he wondered while they continued arranging flowers throughout the sanctuary. For the life of him, he couldn't picture a man appealing enough to catch her interest and stupid enough to let her walk away. Or run, he amended with a frown. You didn't leave a huge, bustling city for the outskirts of Maine without a good reason. He didn't know what had brought her here, but his gut told him it wasn't a pretty story.

Her reluctance to get too close to him was

an obvious hint, but he hated to think about where a clue like that led. It was none of his business anyway, he reminded himself as they wrapped up their floral job. She was Julia's friend, which meant he'd be nice to her but keep a respectable distance. Anything other than that was a complication he didn't need right now.

When he and Lauren met up with Ann in the vestibule, he said, "All set. Did you need anything else?"

"Me? No." Her dark eyes went to Lauren, glimmering with fun. "But since she's here, our guest needs a bonnet for the contest."

"Bonnet contest?" Lauren echoed in a voice normally reserved for the cute blonde in a slasher movie. "What on earth is that?"

"For Easter bonnets," Ann explained as if it was an everyday occurrence everyone should be familiar with. "Julia has so much on her mind these days, she must have forgotten to mention it to you. While the children are off hunting for their eggs, we award a prize for the prettiest ladies' hat."

Judging by the horrified look Lauren gave him, Ben suspected the long-standing tradition hadn't slipped Julia's mind. Knowing what Lauren's reaction would be, she'd purposefully neglected to tell her friend about it. Smart lady.

Hoping to lighten the moment, Ben said, "There was one year it didn't work that way, though. Eddie Wilkins won."

"Oh, that was different," Ann insisted, waving him off. "It's not every day you see a hat with a working toy helicopter on top."

"A helicopter? Are you serious?" Lauren started laughing. It was a bright, happy sound ideally suited to such a beautiful morning, and he was glad to be around to hear it. What would it take, he wondered, to coax it from her again?

"Yeah," he answered with a grin. "It got away from him, though, and someone finally found it in a tree up in Turnberry."

"Very clever," Ann agreed, rubbing her hands together with enthusiasm. "But Lauren doesn't need anything like that. I've got an old gardening hat in the choir room. I'll get that while you two pick out some flowers to put on it." Neither of them moved, and she shooed them with an impatient motion. "Off with you, now. We haven't got all morning."

She hustled off, and Ben turned to Lauren with a shrug. "Around here, she's the boss."

"What about Pastor McHenry?" she asked

as they retraced their steps to pick a few blos-
soms from each display.

"She lets him think he is. I guess that's why
they've been married so long."

"That's how my parents are, too," Lauren
commented in a fond tone. "It seems to work
for them."

Talk of happy parents dimmed the sunny
morning for him, and Ben regretted bringing
up the subject. Fortunately, Ann reappeared
with a broad-brimmed sun hat and saved him
from himself.

"Here we are, dear," she said cheerily, handing it to Lauren. With expert fingers, Ann
took flowers from each of them, threading
the blooms into the faded ribbon that circled
the crown and tied the hat on. When she was
finished, she held it up with an expectant look.
"What do you think?"

Lauren slid him a dubious look, and Ben
answered her unspoken question. "Pretty as
a picture. Try it on."

She nailed him with a glare that could have
frozen the harbor over in July. But for Ann,
she called up a good-sport smile and went
along. Once she'd tied it in place, Ann fussed
with the floral decorations a little and stepped
back for a better look.

"Very nice," she announced with a nod.

"You young folks have cameras on your phones these days. Would you like me to take a picture for you?"

"I don't have mine with me," Lauren replied. "Sorry."

Ben fished out his own and handed it to Ann. "Great idea. When you're done, I'll take one of you two."

While Ann lined up the shot, under her breath Lauren hissed, "I'll get you for this."

Far from intimidated, he chuckled, which only seemed to make her madder.

"I mean it," she assured him.

"I'm sure you do. You're gonna be here awhile, so you'll have plenty of chances."

"Say cheese!"

After Ann snapped a couple more for good measure, Ben looked over Lauren's shoulder at the results. Something about the way they looked together caught him by surprise, and it took him a few seconds to shake off the unexpected reaction. Hoping to sound casual, he smiled at Lauren. "That's a keeper."

Some of the ice in her eyes melted, and she tilted her head at him. "Me or the hat?"

"Both."

Where had that come from? he wondered with a mental groan. He hadn't meant to say it, but it jumped out of his foolish mouth all on its own. He'd have to be more careful around their intriguing guest, or he'd be blurting out all kinds of things he shouldn't.

When they joined everyone out in the square, families were beginning to arrive. The adults greeted each other with hugs and handshakes, while the kids fidgeted in place, anxious for the hunt to start. Ann was in charge of the chaotic event, and when she stood on a chair and clapped her hands, the crowd settled down almost immediately.

The pastor's wife wasn't tall or intimidating in any way, and he'd always marveled at her ability to make people listen to her. He towered over her, but he didn't have half the authority she did. How did you get that, anyway? Maybe one of these days he'd get up the courage to ask her.

"Good morning!" After the gathering returned her greeting, she skimmed the faces with a motherly smile. "I know you're not here to listen to me ramble on, but there are a few rules for our Easter egg hunt. First, no grownups allowed. The children made these eggs, and they've earned the right to find them on their own. Second, the limit is six." Pausing, she aimed a knowing look at several of the older children, who had the decency to squirm. "Third, have fun!"

With that, she threw up her hands, and the race was on. Any adult who didn't want to be crushed by a horde of excited rug rats retreated under an old maple tree, where the bonnet contest was getting underway. Ben was astounded to see who this year's judge was. "Nick McHenry?"

"Put your eyes back in your head," Nick grumbled, his rigid smile doing nothing to mask his disgust. "Julia talked me into doing this."

"I thought Cooper and Bree were the judges this year."

"Mayor and Mrs. Landry had some mysterious last-minute thing this morning," Nick replied in a voice loaded with sarcasm. "Bree called Julia, begging for her help with this nonsense. She knows I hate this town stuff, but she volunteered me anyway, so here I am."

His old buddy was glowering like a troll who'd been dragged out from under his favorite bridge, and Ben couldn't hold back a grin. "When did you get back?"

"Last night," Nick replied with a yawn. "Every time I take a trip, my flights go haywire."

At least you get to go, Ben thought enviously. It wasn't like him to be that way, and he turned his attention to the pretty distraction standing beside him. "You two haven't met yet. Nick McHenry, Lauren Foster."

The fake smile softened into a real one, and Nick held out his hand. "It's great to finally meet you. Thanks for coming to cover the store while we're away."

"I'm happy to do it," she assured him. "Julia's helping me out, too, so it works for everyone."

The comment struck Ben oddly, and he wondered what she meant by it. It seemed the more time he spent with Lauren, the more curious he became about her. Although he made a point of steering clear of complicated women, he was pretty sure she was hiding something—but what? Since he wasn't likely to find that answer anytime soon, he put it aside and scoped out this year's selection of bonnets.

With her love of costumes, Amelia Landry had an extensive collection of extravagant hats. This one looked like it had come straight out of a 1920's movie, except for the flocked rabbits and sheep she'd glued on. That she'd made a miniature version of it for the Pomeranian cradled in her arms was icing on the cake. The Bakery Sisters had gone Western, with matching cowgirl hats that had tiny horses circling the brims. There were plenty of others, from pretty to downright strange, but amid all the craziness, what stood out for him were Lauren's changing expressions.

They went from bewildered to amused, and she gradually got into the playful spirit of the contest. While they waited for Nick to make his choice, she mingled with some of the other entrants, complimenting their taste—or smoothing over the lack of it—with a skill that impressed him. Tightly wound as she seemed at first, once she loosened up, she had a real way with people.

When Hannah bounded over to say hello, Lauren's face lit up as if she'd just reconnected with her long-lost best friend.

"Ben! Lauren!" Out of breath, Hannah held up her basket for them to see. "Look!"

"Awesome," Ben approved then leaned down to murmur, "I think you've got more than six, though."

"Noah's sick, so Gramma said I could get some for him. I didn't want my little brother to miss out."

"That's really sweet of you," Lauren said, hunkering down for a closer look. Carefully nudging the top ones aside, she smiled at the excited little girl. "It looks like you found the best ones."

"I don't want any ugly Easter eggs," Nick's

niece informed her in a very grown-up voice. "I left those for the boys."

Again, Lauren's laughter caught Ben pleasantly off guard, and he noticed Ann watching them from across the lawn. Clearly delighted, she sent him an approving smile before focusing back on Nick and his list. Now that Ben thought about it, she'd been whispering with Amelia over something earlier. With their own sons happily tied down, had they turned their attention to him? It would be just like them, and while he recognized that they meant well, he resolved to nip their matchmaking in the bud. Not that it would work with Lauren, who seemed just as determined as he was to avoid getting wrapped up in anything serious. Still, he didn't want to risk them starting something he had no intention of finishing.

"Okay, everyone," Nick announced loudly, holding up a bronze hat stand with a plaque on the front. "We're set. It was a tough call, but this year's winner of the Bonnet Trophy is Lauren Foster."

He held the trophy out for her, but she whispered, "I can't. These people worked really hard on their hats, and your mother threw this together for me five minutes ago."

A murmur rippled through the crowd, and Nick leaned in to mutter, "It's either you or

Amelia Landry, who's won this thing five years running. She's a real sweetheart, but come on—she made a hat for her dog."

"Actually, I think that's adorable."

Nick didn't move, and when she flashed Ben a "help me" look, he shrugged. "Up to you."

After a moment, she shook her head and accepted her prize. Undoing her hat, she set it on the stand and smiled from Nick to the others gathered around. "Thank you very much."

She was rewarded with a round of applause, and the square quickly emptied out. Ben was thinking it was time to get going when Julia hurried over to where he and Lauren stood chatting with Nick. "We've got a problem."

"What now?" Nick growled. When she tilted her head at him, he backpedaled. "Sorry. What's wrong?"

"We hid four hundred eggs. The kids only found three hundred and forty-two of them."

Sending a horrified look around the large park, Lauren groaned. "Are you telling me there are fifty-eight eggs still here, just waiting to rot and stink up the whole town?"

"And our wedding reception," Julia added, sending Nick an urgent look.

"The raccoons will get them."

Ben thought that made sense, but Julia clearly disagreed. Folding her arms, she gave

Nick a stern glare. "Then we won't know how many might be left. I'm not going anywhere until we've found every last one of them."

Evidently unwilling to go up against his unyielding fiancée, he relented with a glance over at Ben. "Gimme a hand?"

"Sure." Chuckling, Ben draped an arm around his shoulders and angled him toward the gazebo. "Anything to save the wedding."

Easter Sunday dawned bright and beautiful. It was the kind of spring day that made you believe anything was possible, and Ben felt optimistic while he pulled his one suit out of its plastic wrap and dressed for church.

When he reached his father's house, though, his mood dimmed considerably. The truck was gone, and taped to the storm door he found a note:

Gone fishing. See you tomorrow.

Trudging back to his own truck, Ben tried to summon some kind of emotion. Disappointment, anger, something. Sadly, the best he could come up with was ambivalence. The fact that his father had chosen to dodge the Easter service he once looked forward to should have worried Ben, but he couldn't dredge up much of anything other than pity.

While he drove into town, he recognized that over the past few months, the one thing he could count on was that he couldn't rely on his father anymore. Missed meals, disappearing, showing up late and hung over for work—they'd all become things Ben had been forced to accept because he didn't have the first clue about how to change them.

For all intents and purposes, he was single-handedly running Thomas and Sons. Nick had run his own online magazine for years, and he'd often teased Ben that he was way too nice to be the one in charge. Sadly, Ben was beginning to agree with him, but he was a fairly smart guy, and he could figure out a way to remedy the situation. Had to, if the business he depended on for his paychecks was going to continue.

Putting an end to his father walking all over him would be a good start. He'd done everything he knew to keep Dad's spirits up, but judging by his latest vanishing act, it had all been pointless. From his parents' tumultuous relationship, Ben knew some kinds of problems couldn't be solved—they had to be endured. Eventually, you got past them and they faded into the background of your life. They became part of who you were, but they didn't define you anymore.

That thought led him to Lauren, which had been happening a lot since he met her. She was obviously dealing with something of her own, and the hints of strength she'd shown intrigued him more than he cared to admit. She'd initially struck him as the princess type, but he'd caught a few glimpses of a stubborn streak under that polished veneer. Normally, he preferred sweet, uncomplicated women who adored him and weren't shy about telling him so. Lauren's reserve presented a challenge part of him was dying to take on.

The more sensible part of him knew better. As he parked in the crowded church lot and made his way inside, he resolutely put Lauren Foster out of his mind. He knew trouble when he saw it, and her slender frame was packed with it.

When he paused in the entryway, Julia noticed him and motioned to an empty spot beside her. Much as he enjoyed the McHenrys' company, today he needed time to himself to brood without bringing anyone else down. So he waved her off and took a seat in the back row, close to the fresh air and sunshine that had started his day out so nicely.

Unfortunately, it had gone downhill from there. Lately that was just how his days seemed to go.

Chapter Five

$\smile\!\!\sim$

After Julia left for church, Lauren showered and enjoyed a leisurely breakfast with Shakespeare. While he crunched on his designer bird food, she brewed some exotic coffee and warmed up a cinnamon roll that barely fit on a cake plate.

"There are some seriously good cooks in this town," she told the parrot through a mouthful of icing. He eyed her with curiosity, then bobbed his head as if he agreed with her.

"This is the short and the long of it."

"You got that right."

All that sugar and caffeine got her going, and even though it was her day off, she was dying to do something. She'd declined Ann's offer of lunch, so that left her completely to her own devices. She'd spent most of last Sunday trying to process the dire circumstances that had driven her to the ends of the earth. Or the ends of Maine, anyway. After a week decompressing, she thought maybe it was time to devise a plan for when Julia returned from her honeymoon and didn't need her help anymore.

Tuning her mind to a more optimistic frequency, Lauren tried to look past where she was and into the future. Unfortunately, she saw nothing. Nothing yet, she amended in an attempt to keep her fragile spirits up. With a mental shrug, she wandered over to the enormous bay window that overlooked Main Street.

A few cotton-candy clouds were scattered through the sky, filtering the sunlight into long beams that brightened the scene below. Since it was Easter, it didn't take much to imagine that the Almighty Himself had thrown open the gates of heaven to let the light out for a little while. It was too gorgeous a day to waste inside flipping through TV channels, so she grabbed a windbreaker and headed outside.

She didn't have a route in mind, just followed where her feet took her. In New York, she'd never ventured out alone like this, and the freedom was wonderful. The caution hadn't been just for safety, either, she recalled with a frown. Jeremy didn't like to let her out of his sight for longer than absolutely necessary. Thinking back, that was probably why he'd gotten her a job in his law office. It wasn't generosity, she realized now. It was control. The truth came through so clearly today, she couldn't believe it had escaped her before.

Then again, she mused as she strolled down the sidewalk, she'd seen what she wanted to see. With his cover model looks and bottomless bank account, Jeremy Rutledge appeared to be every woman's dream, and Lauren had been more than flattered by his attention. By the time she recognized what she'd gotten herself into, she'd given up the rights to her own life. The only way out was to run, and she'd gone as far as she could without winding up in the Atlantic Ocean. She'd never mentioned Julia to Jeremy, and as each day passed with no word from him, she felt herself relaxing into her new surroundings.

Temporary, she reminded herself, but safe. For someone who'd learned to take things one day at a time, that was enough.

When her wandering took her by the square, she walked up to the flower-draped gazebo and sat on one of the benches inside. Several robins had made nests in the rafters, and they scolded her for invading what they obviously considered their territory. When she noticed some of them were sitting still, she decided they must be guarding their eggs.

Now that she understand what all the ruckus was about, she sneaked out as quietly as she could and continued on her way. The doors of the church were open, and just as she passed the sign, she heard the organist play the opening chords of "Amazing Grace." The congregation sang it with gusto, a pleasant blend of voices that made her stop and listen. By coincidence, she was near the sign, and the words hit her with an impact that startled her. She'd read them before in passing, but for some reason, this time they pulled her up short.

Safe Harbor Church. All are welcome.

Lauren wasn't superstitious, nor was she egotistical enough to presume the world revolved around her. But crazy as it seemed, she couldn't help feeling that someone was trying to tell her something. Bewildered by the sensation, she edged toward the double doors and peered inside. What she saw there made her heart cringe with sympathy.

Ben was sitting in the back, on a single chair pulled far back into the shadows. While the congregation sang, he sat with his arms resting on his knees, staring at his nicely polished shoes. It was a defeated look, totally wrong for the bright, engaging man who always seemed so upbeat. Lauren understood what he was doing, withdrawing from everyone, trying to get lost in a dark corner so no one would notice how much he was hurting. She had no idea what was bothering him, but for it to take him so far down, it must be awful. That he'd come out in public at all told her just how courageous he was, and how seriously he took his faith.

Next thing she knew, she was creeping into the chapel. Lauren hadn't meant to attend the service, so she wasn't exactly dressed for it. But since she was on a mission of mercy, she hoped God would forgive her for wearing jeans and sneakers. The carpet muffled her steps, and when she knelt down beside Ben, he didn't seem to notice. Maintaining personal space was a big deal for her, but she swallowed her fear and rested a hand on the sleeve of his jacket.

He barely registered the gesture, angling his head to give her an irritated look. When he saw it was her, the anger vanished, replaced by an amazed expression. "Lauren?"

Pulling her hand away, she searched for something to say. Her decision to come in had been pure impulse, and she hadn't considered what to do next. Inspiration struck, and she smiled. "Happy Easter."

He echoed her greeting, then stood and motioned for her to take his seat. She nearly refused, but the suddenly brighter look on his face made her think again. Focusing on his problems had made her feel better about her own. Maybe a distraction would work for him, too. So she thanked him and sat, pleased when he hunkered down beside her.

"I thought you were sleeping in today," he whispered. His grin wasn't full-wattage today, but it was still pretty amazing.

"It's too nice for that."

"What made you come in here?"

She didn't want to lie, but the truth would be awkward, at best. So she settled for something reasonable. "I heard the music."

The hymn was over, so he just nodded and turned his attention to the pastor. The sadness that had brought her in seemed to have faded a bit, and Lauren felt the satisfaction of knowing she'd returned some of the kindness Ben had shown her. Since she was here, she decided to stay and see how it went. Everyone was in their best clothes, but she still recognized fishermen, storekeepers and several of Julia's customers. It was an eclectic mix of people, and she marveled at how they'd gathered to worship together.

Julia was up front with the McHenrys, and

when Nick leaned over to say something to her, she smiled and reached over to take his hand. Watching them, Lauren was happy for her old friend, but she also felt a twinge of envy. It seemed Julia had found the ideal way to spend the rest of a long, happy life with Nick. Was it coincidence? Lauren wondered. Or was there more to it?

Philosophy wasn't her strong point, and while she was mulling over the possibilities, Pastor McHenry began his sermon. As if picking up her train of thought, he reminded them all that everyone here was different but with something very important in common. They were all God's children, doing their best to follow His son's example and live a good life.

"On this day," he said, "when we celebrate the resurrection, I pray we all find peace in the knowledge that no matter how many times we've fallen, we can always begin again. The first step is to open our hearts and allow God to guide our steps. With His help, we may falter, but we'll find the courage to regain our footing and move ahead."

Although he was smiling at the congregation in general, those words resonated deep inside Lauren, as if he'd put them together solely to reach her at the back of the chapel. Somehow, this man she'd never met had summed up the past year of her life in a few humble sentences. Glancing around discreetly, she noted a similar reaction on other faces.

That told her she wasn't the only one struggling to get her life on track again, and she felt lighter somehow. It was as if her troubles had been physically weighing her down and some of the burden had been lifted away. How, she had no clue, but the sensation was as odd as it was unexpected, and it made her nervous, to say the least.

She'd done nothing to cause any kind of change, she reasoned as she stood for the final hymn. Standing here in this little white church, her head next to Ben's over a song neither of them was singing very well, she felt as if she'd finally found where she belonged. It wasn't what she'd anticipated finding in Holiday Harbor, but she couldn't deny that it felt right. After all she'd been through, she sank into that feeling with a gratitude that warmed her all the way down to her toes.

When the service was over, Ben stepped back to let Lauren walk out ahead of him. Ann called out his name, and he frowned but quickly replaced it with a patient smile before turning to face her.

"Are you two sure you won't come to lunch?" she asked, looking from him to Lauren. "I hate to think of you alone, eating a sandwich somewhere."

"We won't be," he assured her, slanting Lauren a follow-along look. "Lauren wanted to explore those old sea caves the other day, but the tide was up. I thought I'd take her now so she can get a close-up look at 'em."

His explanation seemed to satisfy the motherly woman, and she nodded. "All right, then. We'll see you soon."

Lauren added her own goodbye and followed Ben outside. When he headed in the direction of the lighthouse, she said, "Hang on a second. We're not going down there."

"We are now," he retorted, as if he wasn't crazy about it, either. "It might not seem like a big deal to you, but I don't lie to people."

His long stride outpaced hers, and she hurried to keep up. "What's that supposed to mean?"

"Nothing. Forget I said it."

His clipped tone made it clear he not only meant it, but he didn't want to discuss why. Not long ago, she'd have taken that kind of comment like a blow, ducking as best she could so it wouldn't land squarely and hurt too much. But in the past few days, she'd begun to feel more like her old self, and she refused to backslide now. "Stop."

Heaving a long-suffering male sigh, he paused on the shoulder beside her and looked down at her. "What?"

"You know what," she spat. "You all but accused me of being a liar, and I want to know what I've done to make you think that."

His jacket was open, and the breeze picked at it, ruffling through the tie he'd loosened as soon as he left the church. He looked much more in his element out here, in the rugged outskirts of the town, and she could picture him out on a boat, enjoying the freedom of a summer day on the water.

The gaze he fixed on her was a puzzling combination of confusion and respect, and she wasn't sure what to make of it. "Don't take this wrong, but you're a lot smarter than I gave you credit for."

Equal parts furious and flattered, she glared at him for all she was worth. "How could I possibly take that wrong?"

Men misjudged her all the time, to the point where she'd actually resigned herself to it. To most of them, she was nothing more than a pretty accessory on their arm, something they wore like a designer watch to make them look good. That Ben had seen past her appearance to her intelligence pleased her immensely. If she hadn't been so mad at him, she'd have complimented him for his perceptiveness.

Giving her a sheepish look, he took a step forward. Then another. He was getting close to violating her comfort zone, but she planted her feet and met his gaze without flinching. Cocking his head, he gave her a slow, approving grin. "I don't scare you anymore, do I?"

"You never did."

Even to her own ears, that sounded more like bravado than courage, but she concentrated on those impossibly blue eyes, trying to ignore the fact that each one held a different twinkle than the other. In the space of a heartbeat, the sparkle clouded over, giving way to a murky bluish-gray color that could only mean trouble.

"Who was he?"

The blunt question caught her off guard, and she blinked in surprise. "Who was who?"

"The guy who made you afraid," he clarified in an understanding voice. "The one who made you run away to a place where he can't find you."

I didn't run away.

Even as the protest flitted through her mind, Lauren knew otherwise. She'd become adept at deceiving herself, soothing her fears with explanations for Jeremy's behavior that had enabled her to stay with him even while his jealousy had spiraled out of control. Instinctively, she knew Ben Thomas would never treat a woman that way. Strong as he was, beneath that strength ran a gentle current that compelled him to be kind to a frightened woman he'd only met a few days ago.

"You don't have to tell me now," he assured her. "But when you're ready, I'm a decent listener with a rotten memory."

Lauren had no idea how to respond to that, so she settled for a shaky nod. Smiling, he let her go ahead of him, and they made their way down to the rocky strip of beach she'd been so anxious to investigate the other day.

"We used to play down here when we were kids," he began with a chuckle. "We'd hide in the caves and spook the tourists."

The story had a nostalgic ring to it, and she was grateful to him for changing the awkward subject they'd been discussing. "Who's *us?*"

"Nick and me and Cooper Landry."

"The mayor who was supposed to judge the bonnet contest?"

"That's him."

"Interesting," she commented with a little smile. "He's gone from scaring off the beachcombers to pulling them in."

"Something like that." Ben shed his jacket

and slung it over his shoulder in the same easy motion he used for everything. She realized she shouldn't be noticing things like that, but she couldn't help herself. He had a fluid, natural grace that made other guys she knew look downright clumsy.

Eyeing the caves as they strolled past, she said, "They don't look all that safe to me."

"Some are okay, but some flood at high tide. You have to know which is which."

"So, if the tide's coming in, head for higher ground. Got it."

"Actually, you're better off steering clear altogether," he cautioned. "Folks get hurt down here all the time, and when they turn up missing, the EMTs have to go out after them."

"Can't they just call for help?"

"Cell service is pretty spotty out here. The smartest thing is to hike with a buddy."

He topped his advice off with a broad grin, and she laughed. "You mean, like you?"

"Well, if you fell and twisted your ankle, I could carry you back to town."

"Good to know."

They walked a little farther, and he pointed to a wide rock formation that resembled a natural bench. "These shoes are way too tight for a long walk. Mind if we stop for a minute?"

They sat together in silence, giving Lauren a

chance to admire the view. They were far from town, and the distant lighthouse perched on its rocky point seemed like it was in another place altogether. Waves rolled in one after the other, crashing over the boulders with a rhythmic sound that made her feel like a speck in the overall scheme of things.

Filling her lungs with the salty air, she sighed. "Amazing."

"I know what you mean," he agreed as he lounged on the rock beside her. "Whenever I get stressed, I come out here and it all seems like nothing."

His confession startled her, and she swiveled to face him. "What stresses you out? I thought you left the hard stuff up to God."

"That doesn't mean nothing bothers me. Being out here—" he nodded toward the sea "—helps me remember that whatever I'm going through will leave eventually, like the tide. My granddad was a fisherman all his life, and he's the one who taught me life is always in motion. We can't change that, so we just have to ride out the storms the best we can."

The homespun wisdom settled nicely into Lauren's ears, and she smiled. "He sounds like a pretty smart guy."

"He was," Ben agreed with a fond smile. "He died a few years ago, and I miss him every day. I think he was the one holding our family together. After we lost him, everything started going haywire."

Judging by the tone of his voice, Lauren assumed he didn't realize she didn't know his history the way everyone else in town did. It was an awkward moment, and she wasn't sure how to handle it, so she kept quiet.

After a few moments of quiet, he grimaced. "Sorry, I forgot you don't know much about me. My parents' marriage was never the best, but last year Mom took off with a sales rep she met in a nearby town. The divorce went through a few days ago, and now my dad's MIA."

"Oh, Ben, I'm so sorry." Without thinking, she reached out to rub his shoulder. The gesture was so unlike her, she was startled by how easily she did it. "Holidays like this must be really tough on you two."

"Yeah. Folks mean well, but when they invite me over, it just reminds me what a mess my own family is."

Lauren flashed back to her momentary envy of Julia and Nick, and she could relate to how he must feel. Her own parents had their problems, but they always managed to talk them through and come to some kind of compromise. Ben's situation made her appreciate them even more.

Then the end of what he'd said registered, and she asked, "You told me Thomas and Sons was just you and your father. How do you run the business all by yourself?"

"Lots of juggling and late nights."

The cavalier response did nothing to mask his frustration, and she scowled. "That's not fair. I mean, I understand he's upset, but that doesn't excuse him for leaving you with all that work."

"I know," Ben sighed. "But he's my dad. What'm I supposed to do?"

Although she'd had plenty of trouble sticking up for herself, like most people, Lauren had no problem whatsoever identifying someone else's options. "Would you let any other employee get away with what he's doing?"

"I'm not sure. I've never been a boss before." When she tilted her head at him, he gave her a wry grin. "I guess I wouldn't."

"What would you do?"

"Talk to him, let him know what he's doing is wrong."

His answer came slowly, as if it pained him to say the words, and she reminded herself they were discussing his father. "That's a good start, but I think you need to tell him what's going to happen if he doesn't straighten him-self out."

Ben let out a long, painful groan. "I can't fire my own father. It's his company."

"Judging by how exhausted you look now, you'll be out of business by fall. You need to be tough with him, or he'll just keep walking all over you." His dubious expression clearly said he wasn't convinced. Changing tactics, she homed in on something she knew Ben wanted badly enough to take a stand. "If you get him back on track and hire some new guys, you can take one of those restoration jobs you were talking about."

That did it. Hope glimmered in Ben's eyes, and he pinned her with a deadly serious look. "Ya think?"

"I can't be sure, but I know one thing—if your dad can't operate on his own, your dreams will stay on hold. Maybe forever."

She added the last bit for some extra spice, and it had the effect she was after. Ben's jaw tightened and steel glinted in his eyes. "It makes me mad every time I think about it. There's a plum job in Boston starting in June, but I'm stalling on an answer 'cause I couldn't live with myself if I let him down."

That was so sad, she thought. Ben was a good guy, and his sense of loyalty had trapped him in a place he no longer wanted to be. Unfortunately, she could relate to that. "Having you to lean on may actually be handicapping him. If you go, he might learn to stand on his own two feet again."

Staring out at the water, Ben fell silent, and she let him be. Solutions were so obvious when it was someone else's life, she thought with a sigh. If only she could fix her own as easily.

"Well," he said as he stood up and brushed off his trousers, "I'd best be getting home. How 'bout you?"

"Sounds good. I haven't called my parents in a few days, so I should check in with them."

Ben pulled his offending shoes back on, and they began walking up the path. "I'd like to meet them. Are they coming up for the wedding?"

"They wanted to, but my younger sister's baby is due at the beginning of May. It's her first, so she's pretty nervous about going through labor, not to mention taking care of an infant afterward. Mom's going to be in the delivery room, just in case they need some expert hand-holding. Then she'll do the doting grandma thing when they come home from the hospital."

"What about your dad? Is he the pacing-out-in-the-waiting-room type?"

She laughed at the mere idea that Don Foster might be left out of his grandchild's grand entrance into the world. "Oh, he's the cameraman. A Hollywood movie set doesn't have as much equipment as he does."

"I was like that after my niece was born," Ben commented with a smile. "Allie's a lot like Hannah, a real tomboy with plenty of sugar on top."

After his sobering family news, the upbeat topic seemed to restore his normal optimism. Picking up on that, she asked him questions that led to some cute stories and laughter over the funny things kids do. By the time they got back to town, she felt as if they'd made some kind of breakthrough in their unforeseen new friendship. For her, men were dates, not buddies, and this was a novel experience for her.

In the doorway of Toyland, she turned to him and smiled. "Thanks for walking me back."

"No problem."

When she unlocked the knob and tried to turn it, it stuck a little, and before she knew what was happening, Ben's hand reached past hers to twist open the stubborn mechanism. He wasn't touching her, but he was way too close for comfort, and she stiffened reflexively.

"I'm not gonna hurt you, Lauren. I promise."

The tone of his voice was reassuring, but she flashed back to their earlier conversation and closed her eyes to avoid looking at him. "I haven't even told Julia what happened. How did you know?"

"Just a hunch," he replied as he stepped away. He seemed to realize she needed space, and for that she was incredibly grateful. "But I want you to know you're safe here with us."

Lauren noticed her reflection in the glass door and was disgusted by the terrified look on her face. Taking a deep breath, she asked, "By us, do you mean with the town or with you?"

"Yes."

Offering her a smile of encouragement in the window, he turned and strolled across the street to where his truck was alone in the lot. His easy acceptance of her baffling behavior soothed Lauren's frazzled nerves, and she found herself staring after him. Could it be she'd stumbled onto a truly good man who respected her wishes? One who wouldn't try to manipulate or bribe her into doing what he wanted?

It was hard to believe, but while she made her way upstairs, it was the only explanation she could come up with. As she rounded the top step, Shakespeare called out, "A horse! A horse! My kingdom for a horse!"

Thanks to him, Lauren was laughing when her dad picked up the phone.

"Something's funny?" he asked, his smile obvious over the long-distance connection.

"Julia's bird-sitting this hilarious macaw." She described the parrot to him, adding in a few entertaining lines from his repertoire. "I'm just calling to wish you a Happy Easter. Is Mom there, too?"

"On the other line," she answered. "How are things going up there?"

"It's a lot different from what I'm used to, but I'm getting the hang of it."

Actually, she loved it, especially the children she'd been hanging out with. They were cute and funny, and she even enjoyed the shy ones, coming up with ways to draw them into a conversation. Not ready yet to tell them she might be staying, instead she described the old building and how her friend had given it new life as a toy store.

"It sounds like a lot of work," Dad commented. "How did she manage all that?"

"She has an incredibly talented contractor who's good at all kinds of things."

"Really?" her mother asked.

She was a teen counselor, and she had the

sharpest ears on the planet. Lauren had done her best to keep the comment casual, but judging by her mom's suddenly alert tone, she hadn't quite managed it. In all fairness, she thought with a grin, it was tough to stay neutral when it came to the outgoing carpenter. "His name is Ben Thomas, and he's a good friend of hers."

"What do you know about him?" her father growled.

"Oh, Don," Mom chided, "do you really think Julia would allow someone to come around if he wasn't completely trustworthy?"

"Well, no," he admitted grudgingly. "But I don't like it."

"Always the cop," she chided in a fond voice. "Lauren meets new people all the time, and she handles them just fine. Don't you, sweetheart?"

Mostly, Lauren replied silently. To her parents, she said, "Ben's very nice, the perfect gentleman. Even Shakespeare likes him."

Why she added that last part, she had no idea, but it had the effect she was looking for. Dad laughed, and she could imagine him shaking his head. As the only male in a houseful of women, he'd always done that a lot. He probably figured it was better than screaming. "Okay, but if he gives you any trouble, tell him your dad's a cop with FBI connections. That'll give him something to think about."

Somehow, she couldn't imagine the FBI threat having much effect on the cocky handyman, but she appreciated her father's gesture anyway. "I'll do that. Talk to you soon."

In unison, they said, "Love you, honey."

After hanging up, Lauren connected her phone to the charger and slumped down on the sofa to stare at the ceiling. All her parents knew was that she and Jeremy had broken up about a month ago, and she was relieved they'd never been nosy enough to ask her for details. Neither of them had mentioned Jeremy calling them, which was good. The more she considered it, though, it seemed odd because he hadn't tried to contact her, either. Did that mean he didn't care that she'd left, or was he giving her time to stew about their future confrontation?

Because, much as she'd like to believe otherwise, she knew they'd have it out eventually. She only hoped she was up to the challenge.

Chapter Six

Monday morning, Ben resisted the urge to go check on his father before heading out to put the finishing touches on a customer's new screened-in porch. He never showed up or called, and Ben focused his attention on the job to keep from worrying. Tuesday ran the same way, and he continued working at the lighthouse by himself. By noon on Wednesday he was no longer worried.

He was furious.

Lauren was right, he finally admitted, ripping damaged shingles from the roof with more force than was strictly necessary. His father was taking advantage of the situation, confident Ben would cover his absences with his own overtime. All because he knew his son didn't have anything better to do, Ben groused while he powered up his circular saw to remove the rotten wood beneath layers of old patches.

Well, no more, he resolved, as he lowered his safety glasses and started cutting. He couldn't do much about it now, but by the time his dad bothered to show his face in town again, he'd have a plan. And it wouldn't involve Ben killing himself to keep the family business going. If Dad didn't care about it, why should he?

By the time he was done on the roof, he'd worked out most of his temper with his hammer. But when he entered the lighthouse residence, Mavis met him in the hallway with a cup of apple cider and a plate of gingerbread.

Giving him a rare look of sympathy, she said, "You need to take a break before you stomp right through what's left o' my roof."

"Sorry."

"Come sit down a minute," she suggested, leading the way into the parlor. "You're scaring Reggie half to death."

A muffled grunting came from behind a chair, and Ben saw the tail end of her miniature pig wriggling into the corner. He felt awful for frightening the little guy, and he snapped off a piece of gingerbread. Sitting on the floor, he held it out like a peace offering. "Noisy stuff's done, boy. Come on out."

That got him a questioning grumble, and he put a cork in his dark mood. Chuckling, he answered, "Promise."

It was a tight squeeze, but the little porker managed to back himself out and give Ben a cautious look. When he caught a whiff of the snack, all was forgiven, and he curled up in Ben's lap to enjoy his treat. Thankfully, Mavis didn't press him to tell her what had him so upset. Probably because, like everyone with eyes and a brain, she could figure it out for herself.

They chatted about the weather, how bad the fishing was this time of year, even Nick and Julia's upcoming wedding. Everything but his father, which Ben appreciated.

"Y'know what you need?" she asked with a knowing look.

She'd been so great about his temper tantrum, he decided to play along. "What's that?"

"A girlfriend." He opened his mouth to protest that he had plenty of them, and she waved him off. "Not the girls around here. They're all half in love with you already, and there's no challenge in that. You need a woman who's seen some of the world and doesn't like it much. Someone who'll look at you and see more than Craig Thomas's fair-haired boy."

Ben had a pretty good idea where this was

headed, and he laughed. "You sound like Amelia Landry. She wants me to ask Lauren Foster out, just for fun."

"Now, I don't normally agree with that ball of fluff," Mavis assured him, "but this time, I think she's right. Life can be hard, and you should have some fun while you're still young."

The flinty advice came with a dash of fondness, and he grinned. "That sounds like something Granddad would say."

Her lined face broke into a delighted grin, and her pale eyes crinkled with their own approval. "You're a good boy, but I think that's the nicest thing you've ever said to me."

"I mean it." Gently lifting Reggie to set him on his threadbare rug, Ben stood and kissed Mavis's cheek. "I'll finish up your ceiling— quietly—and get outta here. I'm thinking maybe I should stop in at Toyland on my way home."

"That's the way. Nothing much ever comes from folding your hands and waiting for things to line up your way, y'know."

"Yeah," he agreed with a smile. "I know."

Compared to the roofing work, the ceiling repair was a cakewalk, and Ben was finished by two. Mavis had dozed off reading a novel, so Ben slipped out the front door, using the spare key she'd given him to lock it behind him.

On his way into town, he had to stop behind a school bus on Main Street. While he waited for the kids to get off, he looked around absently and noticed Lauren in one of the display windows at Toyland. The space was empty, and she was studying it with her arms folded in a serious-thinking pose. Once the bus got going again, he made a U-turn and parked in front of the store.

She was concentrating so hard, she didn't notice him at first. He raised a knuckle to tap on the glass, then recalled how jittery she got when she was surprised. So instead he waited patiently for her to look up, then he waved. She returned the gesture with a puzzled expression and climbed down to meet him outside.

"Hey, there," he said, trying to sound casual. "How's your day going?"

"Fine. Yours?"

"I finished up out at the lighthouse early, so my day's over."

"That's good." After a pause, she asked, "Did you need something?"

Come on, Ben, an insistent voice in the back of his mind urged. *Ask her to dinner. The worst she can say is no.* "Actually, I wanted to thank you for the great advice you gave me on

Sunday. About my dad," he clarified, in case she'd forgotten their conversation.

"You worked things out with him?"

"Not yet, but I will." Forging ahead, he said, "Ann McHenry stopped by with a ton of leftovers from Easter dinner. Ham, potatoes, homemade rolls, stuff like that. There's no way I can eat it all by myself, so I was hoping you might come by later and give me a hand."

"Eating your leftovers?" Her eyes narrowed suspiciously. "Are you serious?"

That wasn't the reaction he expected, but she'd been startling him since the day he met her. "Sure. I mean, it's not like a date or anything. Just a couple friends sharing some good food before it spoils."

"So we're friends?"

Her expression was unreadable, and he couldn't tell if she was yanking his chain or not. Then he caught the faint quiver at the corner of her mouth, and he decided to join in the game. "Aren't we?"

She chewed on that for a couple seconds then laughed. "I'm not sure what we are, but I guess that comes close enough. What time?"

The sudden burst of laughter from this very serious woman had knocked him for a loop, and his mind went completely blank. "What time what?"

"What time for dinner? Unless you've changed your mind in the last ten seconds."

"Not a chance," he assured her quickly. Realizing that might sound desperate—which of course he wasn't—he summoned a careless grin. "I'm done for the day, so whatever works for you is good with me."

"Julia's due back around six-thirty to take over until we close at nine. How about seven?"

"Seven's great. See you then."

Not wanting to create the impression that he was reluctant to go, he quickly turned and headed for his truck.

"Ben?" He glanced back to find her staring after him with a give-me-a-break kind of look. "Where do you live?"

Smooth, he groaned silently before rattling off his address. She'd really thrown him off his stride, this lost girl from the big city. While he'd done his best to keep his distance, something about her kept drawing him closer, step by helpless step. As he got into his truck and started the engine, he met his own eyes in the rearview mirror and sighed.

He'd tried, really he had. Merging with the light traffic, he consoled himself with the knowledge that, while he'd been unable to resist Lauren's charms, in a month or so she'd be leaving Holiday Harbor. Then his life would go back to the way it was before he knew she existed.

That should have eased his mind, and with any other woman, it would have. For some reason, this time it just made him feel sad.

"Dinner with Ben?" Looking up from the display of doll clothes she was straightening, Julia's eyes danced with obvious delight. "How nice."

"Leftovers," Lauren clarified while she changed out her pearl earrings for more casual hoops. They'd look better with the jeans and polo shirt she was wearing. Not that it mattered, but she didn't want to show up at Ben's looking like she was headed to the opera. "It's not a date or anything."

"I don't care what you call it, it's still nice. He likes you," she added, as if that made a difference.

"I helped him out with a problem, and he's thanking me with ham. No biggie."

Julia's forehead wrinkled with sudden concern. "What kind of problem? He's not in trouble, is he?"

Lauren was fairly certain he didn't want her spreading his dilemma around, so she kept it vague. "No, just a business thing. Speaking of which, I had an idea while I was clearing out the display windows this afternoon."

"Wonderful! Shoot."

Taking that as a good sign, Lauren sat on a nearby child's chair. "The kids had such a great time doing the eggs, I was wondering how we could do that kind of thing more often. That way, they don't just buy toys here—they have fun here, too."

"I like it so far."

The brainstorm had come from nowhere, and Lauren still wasn't sure it was a stroke of genius or just a plain old stroke. Taking a deep breath, she gathered her courage and plowed on. "What if we had playtime? For the girls, we could do up a stage and a big wardrobe filled with costumes, maybe call it Princess Playtime. For boys, we could set up an area of the store like a construction zone, with a big sandbox and lots of tractors, trucks, maybe pieces for a model city they could build however they want."

Julia replied with a noncommittal hum, but Lauren could almost hear the wheels spinning in her friend's agile mind. Rushing ahead, Lauren added, "We could even do birthday parties, which would be great because when the parents drop their kids off and pick them up, they'd probably stop to browse around the store. Not only would you make the money from the party, but you'd sell a few toys at the same time."

When Lauren paused for breath, Julia laughed. "Are you finished?"

"Well, it's just an idea—"

"I love it," Julia interrupted firmly, embracing her for good measure. "It's brilliant, and will set us apart from other shops in the area that just offer their customers shelves full of merchandise. This is just the kind of thing I want for Toyland."

Julia thought her idea was brilliant. Not lame or a waste of time, but brilliant. Lauren's heart soared with excitement, and she barely resisted the urge to clap her hands like an ecstatic two-year-old. "I'm glad you like it."

Tilting her head in that graceful dancer's pose, Julia gave her a regal smile. "I said I love it, and I meant every word. Since it's your concept, I want you to put it together while Nick and I are gone. Then when I get back, I'll have a wonderful surprise waiting for me."

Lauren's enthusiasm dimmed a little, but she gave herself a mental shake. Since graduating from college, she'd longed for the chance to do something entirely on her own but hadn't found the right situation. Julia was offering her a golden opportunity, and she wasn't about to turn it down because it was a little scary. Okay, a lot scary, but that didn't mean she couldn't make it work.

"We'll need some things built," she pointed out. "The stage and storage for all the costumes and toys. Not to mention we have to buy all that stuff to get started."

"Ben's very creative, and he'll give us a good price on the carpentry work. You can get supplies from any of our vendors, and they'll just invoice us the way they normally do. Anything special, set up a new account and we'll pay the bills when they come in."

"Are you sure about this?" Lauren asked hesitantly. "It could add up to a fair amount."

"It will bring in even more than we spend—I'm sure of it." Resting a hand over Lauren's, she continued. "I have faith in you, Lauren. Your playtime idea will be a fabulous addition to Toyland."

Her playtime idea. Lauren rolled the words around in her head a few times, savoring the way they sounded. Beyond that, they made her feel proud of herself for the first time in months, reminding her of just how far she'd fallen before finally seeing the light.

No more of that, she vowed. From here on out, those dark memories were in the past, and the future was filled with sunshine.

Thoughts of sunshine reminded her of Ben, which nudged her to her feet. Although her talk with Julia had been everything she'd hoped for, it had made her late for dinner. "I have to get going. See you later?"

"Eventually," Julia replied with a sigh. "After I close up here, Nick and I are helping Ann choose the music to use during the ceremony. She's come up with twenty pieces and can't decide, so I think it's going to be a long night."

It sounded like torture to Lauren, and she teased, "You could always elope."

From his special perch back in Julia's office, Shakespeare called out, "We could always elope!"

He'd changed the wording slightly, but it was too close to be a coincidence. "There's no way he got that from me. I've only said it once."

"Nick's not crazy about all the hoopla that comes with marrying the daughter of an ambassador, so he taught Shakespeare that to irritate me. He thinks it's hilarious."

Judging by her smile, Julia thought it was pretty funny herself. They made quite the pair, Lauren thought as she went out the front door and headed for Ben's place. Someday, she hoped she'd find a guy who complemented her as well as Nick did Julia.

When she reached the address on Elm Street Ben had given her, Lauren paused to check the scrap of paper. Even when she'd confirmed that yes, she was in the right spot, she couldn't believe her eyes. She'd expected a smallish house that needed some work, maybe some scraggly plants in the garden.

Even at dusk, the house was impressive. A grand Victorian, it rose up behind a rusty wrought-iron fence falling down around an overgrown yard that cried out for a Weed-wacker and some serious hedge trimming. Still, some determined daffodils and tulips were pushing through the layers of old leaves and long grass, proving that at one point, someone had cared enough to plant flowers there.

The home itself had a dignified look to it, and she pictured some long-ago captain's wife on the upper balcony, waving a lace hand-kerchief to her husband as he made his way home from being out at sea. Wide, welcoming porches invited people to stay and visit awhile, and while its white paint was faded and peeling, intricate gingerbread adorned every inch of the sweeping rooflines. The gray shingles appeared to be new, but the clapboard siding looked like it had seen better days. She envisioned it painted blue, and smiled when she noticed the swatch of pale blue on the end wall.

To her mind, this was a family home, minus the family, and it was the last thing she'd expected to find at the other end of her short walk.

While she was mulling that over, Ben appeared in the open screen door, wiping his hands on a towel. "You wanna come in?"

"Sure." Realizing she'd been gawking at his house, she felt compelled to offer an explanation as she went inside. She couldn't come up with anything plausible other than, "This is a really nice place."

"Too nice for a guy who lives by himself, you're thinking," he filled in with a grin. "I grew up one street over, and I always loved this old place. When the owner died and it went up for auction, I scraped together everything I had to buy it. Now I'm fixing it up a little at a time."

"Sort of like on-the-job-training for a historical restoration project?"

"Kinda," he admitted sheepishly. "Would you like a tour?"

"Absolutely."

The cosmetic issues outside paled in comparison to the disaster zone inside the old house's walls. From wallboard to ceilings, everything had been stripped back to the studs, and architect-type sketches and measurements were penciled everywhere. The floors were covered in heavy paper, which led her to believe there was something under it that Ben considered worth saving.

"How old is it?" she asked.

"Built in 1852. I found a bunch of old papers and books in the attic, and near as I can tell, the guy who built it was the captain of a merchant ship that sailed in and out of here back then."

"I thought so," she murmured without thinking. When he gave her a puzzled look, she felt herself blushing. "It's silly, but when I saw it, I was imagining a woman on that upper balcony, welcoming her husband home from a long stint at sea."

"Seriously?" She nodded, and he shook his head. "That's what I used to picture, too. How weird is that?"

Very, Lauren answered silently. So far, she hadn't come up with anything they had in common beyond Julia. That they shared something so bizarre was unsettling, to say the least.

He broke the odd mood with his usual optimism. "I know it's a mess right now, but someday it'll be amazing."

"Are you going to live here or sell it?"

"It's too much house for me, so I'll probably end up selling it," he replied while they walked into the brightly lit kitchen in progress. With tall ceilings and a long bank of windows, it looked out on the yard on two sides. When the gardens were in full bloom, it would look and smell wonderful. "Lots of folks who visit here come back later and end up staying. They love old houses with tons of character."

"This definitely fits the bill." Sitting on a battered stool in front of the butcher block island, she looked around with new appreciation for his carpentry skills. "You're doing a lot more than rebuilding this place. You're bringing it back to life."

Opening the oven, he pulled out a pan with honey-drizzled ham that made her stomach growl impatiently. "I like how that sounds. You wanna do my PR?"

"Oh, I'm no good at things like that," she responded, waving the idea away. "My business degree didn't teach me anything practical."

That seemed to get his attention, and when he was done basting the ham, he fixed her with a somber look. "Why's that?"

"I'm not sure," she confessed slowly. "I just

wasn't into it, I guess. Even a semester in London didn't help much."

"Right. Were you studying or partying?"

"Well—"

"Is that where you met Julia?"

This guy was way sharper than he appeared to be, with his shock of unruly blond hair and endless collection of aw-shucks grins. But his demeanor was more curious than aggressive, and she decided to follow the conversation where it led.

"We literally bumped into each other at a little bistro near Buckingham Palace," she recalled with a smile. "When she found I wanted to see it but had missed the tour, she took me in herself. When one of the dukes found out Julia was there, he came down and greeted us personally. After giving us a private tour, he chatted with us over tea like he had all the time in the world. It was incredible."

Ben let out a low whistle. "I guess so. I've seen pictures of that place, and it's like a museum."

"Tell me about it. I'd never been anywhere outside of Pennsylvania, and Julia took me everywhere. Rome, Vienna, we even had lunch at the top of the Eiffel Tower. Just like in the movies, you can see the whole city from up there."

"Whoa! How cool was that?"

"The coolest. Julia's the best friend I've ever had," Lauren added emphatically. "When I asked if I could come up here for a while, she didn't even blink. She offered me a job and a place to stay, no questions asked."

She hadn't meant to say that last part out loud, and she hoped he wouldn't press her for details she wasn't prepared to share. While she held her breath, she thought he looked like he wanted to say something, but was interrupted by the oven timer. *Saved by the bell,* she thought. While he was busy with the hot food, she stood and went to the fridge. Inside was a salad and a pitcher of iced tea, so she added them to the dinner he was arranging on the island.

When everything was ready, he sat down across from her and held out his hands. "Like they say in France, *bon appétit.*"

She laughed. "For a Maine contractor, you've got a pretty good French accent."

"I'd love to go to Europe someday," he confided around a mouthful of scalloped potatoes. "Those countries have been around so long, you can get a view of history just from studying the architecture."

He said it with such longing, Lauren found herself wishing she could do something to help him make it happen. He was such a good guy—he deserved to have some of his dreams come true. To her surprise, she heard herself say, "You'll get there. And when you do, it'll be worth the wait."

Where had that come from? she wondered. These days, it was all she could do to keep moving forward, one painful step at a time. It had been so long since she'd felt hopeful about anything, the emotion startled her.

"I'm sure you're right about that," he said. "In the meantime, this place oughta keep me busy enough."

They ate for a few minutes in silence, and she suddenly remembered the mission Julia had given her. Setting down her fork, she began, "I had an idea for Toyland."

That got his attention, and his eyes glittered with interest. "Yeah?"

While she outlined what she and Julia had discussed earlier, she could hear the wheels spinning in his head. This man wasn't meant for cement and shingles, she thought wistfully. He was meant to create beautiful things people would enjoy for generations to come. When she was finished, she sat back and folded her hands on the counter. "So what do you think?"

"It's fantastic," he answered without hesitation. "Kids around here will line up for playtime at Toyland."

"I need your help to make it happen, though. Julia doesn't want anyone but you working in her building, and after seeing what you can do, I agree with her. Do you have time?"

"I'll make time."

Jumping from his stool, he grabbed a magnetic pad and pen from its spot on the fridge. While she detailed what she had in mind, he sketched her concept into some kind of primitive blueprint. After a few false starts, they finally settled on something they both liked.

"Excellent," he announced, holding up his hand for a high five. Then he pulled his cell phone from the pocket of his jeans and opened the contacts screen. "I'll add your number in, so I can reach you if I have questions while I'm drafting the plans."

The seemingly innocent request knocked her off her stride, and she did her best to answer without raising suspicion. "You can just call me at the store."

Unfortunately he must have caught the hitch in her voice, because he gave her a long, serious look. "I thought you just left it behind the day of the egg hunt. You really don't have a cell phone?"

"No."

"Why not?"

She could have lied, but he'd been so kind

to her, he deserved better than that. While she was debating how to explain her situation, he leaped ahead in her story and scowled. "Because of *him,* right? The guy you ran away from?"

Suddenly, she was tired of concealing the truth of her situation from everyone. Ben had already guessed the basics, so she decided there was no sense in trying to keep up the charade any longer. "Jeremy." Lauren heard the tremor in her voice and swallowed to steady it. "His name is Jeremy."

"Does he have a last name?"

It was a reasonable question, but the fury blazing in Ben's eyes made her hesitate. The Rutledge family was well-known in New York, and she didn't want Ben doing something foolish like hunting Jeremy down to confront him. So she kept the name to herself and continued. "I met him at a Penn State football game. He was there with friends, and we hit it off. We started dating—me going up to New York, him coming to Philly when he could get away. After a while, I was doing most of the traveling, so he invited me to move in with him."

Pausing, she looked over to gauge Ben's reaction to that. Disapproval darkened his usually mellow features, but he didn't say anything. "I'm not proud of it, but I was so in love with him, I just wanted us to be together. He had a really nice apartment near Central Park, and he got me a job at his office. For a while, it was great."

She stopped to gather her thoughts, and he gently prodded, "Then it wasn't so great."

"We started fighting, about little things at first, then about everything. He didn't want me going anyplace without him, which wasn't a big deal, since I didn't have any friends of my own there anyway. On the rare times we were apart, I discovered he was keeping tabs on where I went and what I did."

"By tracking your cell phone?"

This guy didn't miss a trick, she thought with envy. If only she'd been that savvy, she wouldn't have gotten into this mess in the first place. "Anyway, I finally had enough of that and told him I was going to get an apartment with a friend from college. He didn't take that well."

Unconsciously, she raised a hand to the cheek that still stung whenever she thought about Jeremy. The bruise had faded, but she was convinced the memory of that horrible night would be with her forever.

Rage flooded Ben's eyes, and he fisted his hands on the butcher block as if he were struggling to maintain control of his temper. "I'm glad you didn't tell me his last name, or I'd be on a plane to New York so fast...."

Lauren knew violence wasn't the cure to violence, but the protectiveness seething in his voice was comforting somehow. Just knowing Ben was more than willing to stand between her and the big, bad world made her feel safer than she had in a long time.

Since she'd gone this far, she forged ahead to finish her sad story. "I never told Jeremy about Julia, so it made sense to come here. One day after he left for an early meeting at work, I shredded my credit cards, wiped the memory from my phone and canceled the account. I left behind everything he gave me, bought a plane ticket with cash and came to Holiday Harbor." Now that she was removed from that awful day, she could hardly believe she'd felt compelled to behave so outlandishly. "Looking back, it was surreal, like a movie. I still can't believe I was that paranoid."

"Just 'cause you're paranoid doesn't mean someone's not after you," he assured her gently. "That guy sounds dangerous to me. You were smart to take off and even smarter to cover your tracks."

They barely knew each other, so Ben's approval shouldn't mean that much to her. But it did. While it seemed woefully inadequate, she gave him a grateful smile. "Thanks."

"You're welcome. Now, back to this Playtime area."

Apparently, he'd sensed her desire to change the subject, and again she marveled at his ability to respect her wishes. While they tossed ideas around, she gradually found herself warming to the project—and its contractor.

Wonderful as he seemed, she promised herself that this time she'd be more careful. When you trusted someone with your heart too easily, it could all go bad in a hurry. She wasn't about to make that mistake again.

Chapter Seven

Ben finished out the week as a one-man crew. While his customers were too polite to say anything directly, he couldn't miss the sympathy on their faces and the extra effort they made to compliment his work. That he was dependable and top-notch seemed to be the general consensus, and he was grateful for their attempts to make him feel better about the awkward situation he found himself in. Parents were supposed to smooth over their kids' bad behavior, he grumbled to himself more than once. Not the other way around.

Sunday morning, he left for church a little earlier than normal. Glancing down, he made sure the note he'd labored over was on the seat beside him. Ben would prefer to have it out in person, but if his dad was still away, the stern letter would have to do. He'd had a long, difficult week, and he knew some of his exhaustion stemmed from the frustrating situation with his father.

The only bright spot had been Lauren, he mused with a smile. It turned out they had more in common than he'd have considered possible only a few days ago. Their shared love of history and old buildings was an unexpected—and pleasant—surprise to him. He couldn't help wondering if she felt the same way. Like Ben, she was planning to leave Holiday Harbor for somewhere else. If things continued to go well between them, maybe their paths could intersect once in a while and they'd find a way to remain friends.

His parents' wreck of a marriage made Ben wary of long-term commitments, and Lauren had made it clear she wasn't interested in anything serious. Something else they saw eye to eye on, he thought as he pulled onto Harbor Street. From the far end, he saw his father's truck parked in the driveway, and he gripped the steering wheel a little tighter. While he'd hoped to have this out face-to-face, now that it was reality, second thoughts began creeping in to test his resolve.

In his mind, he heard Lauren's voice. *Would you let any other employee get away with what he's doing?*

Not in a million years, he decided, bracing himself as he left his truck and knocked on the glass in the storm door. The Gone Fishing message was still there, as if Dad was leaving his options open. Unfortunately, Ben didn't have that luxury, and it wasn't much of a struggle to look grim when the door opened.

"Good morning," his father said, stepping back to let him in. "Want some coffee?"

"No, thanks. I'm on my way to church."

"That's right…it's Sunday." Rubbing his stubbled chin, he grimaced. "Think I'll skip it today."

"You've been skipping a lot lately," Ben pointed out as calmly as he could. He didn't want to fight—he just wanted to make sure he said his piece. "I think you should take next week off and figure out what you want to do."

"What do you mean?" his father asked with a confused frown.

He really didn't get it, and Ben nearly lost his stomach for this conversation. He recognized that his dad was in pain, and he'd never intended to hurt his own son. But intentions didn't mean much when the end result was so bad.

Trying to view him as just another unreliable worker, Ben said, "I can't count on you, and I can't go on covering for you the way

I've been doing. You need to get some help for your own sake, but also so we can keep the business going."

"I'm feeling better now," he insisted without much conviction. "We'll be fine."

"Not if you don't find someone to talk to about this." Taking a deep breath, Ben pulled out the final stop. "Davy's holding a spot on his restoration crew for me, and the job starts June 1. You need to get yourself straightened out by Memorial Day, because I'm going to Boston."

Dad's mouth dropped open in total shock, and he slowly shook his head. "How can you even think of doing that to me?"

The accusation felt like a knife plunging into his heart, and while it was exactly what his father had suggested that night up at Schooner Point, Ben knew it was pointless to remind him of it. He also knew this was the only way to demonstrate how deadly serious he was about his father getting help with his problems. Hard as it was, he held his ground. "I've been patient for six months, while you went from giving up on Mom one day to being convinced she'd be home tomorrow. Every time, the low got a little lower, until you disappeared for a whole week. No phone calls, nothing."

"I left you a note."

The lame argument only added fuel to Ben's simmering temper. Summoning every ounce of frustration he'd been accumulating, he finished his speech with a glare. "If you wanna run your life into the ground, that's your business. I'm not sticking around to watch."

With that, he turned on his heel and stalked back to his truck. As he peeled out of the gravel driveway, he resisted the temptation to check the rearview mirror to gauge the reaction his parting shot had caused.

Because, in all honesty, he simply didn't care anymore.

It wasn't far to Safe Harbor Church, and by the time he arrived, he still had a full head of steam. Not the best way to enter God's house, he reminded himself, and he paused in the vestibule to regain his composure. He was considering taking a seat in the back again when he caught a movement in the front pew.

Lauren.

Wearing a pale blue dress dotted with flowers, she looked ready for a leisurely afternoon in someone's garden. All she needed to complete the image was a picnic basket and a blanket. Her beautiful smile wiped away the awful start to his morning, and he joined her in the McHenry clan's usual spot. Taking the seat beside her, he said, "Hey there, sunshine."

With a feminine smirk, she lifted one perfect brow. "What did you call me?"

"You look like sunshine this morning. It seemed to fit."

"I've had a lot of nicknames over the years," she commented quietly. "I think that's my favorite."

Score one for me, Ben thought with a grin. "So, what brings you here?"

"I liked what I saw on Easter Sunday. I thought I'd see how it plays from the front."

Ben didn't care why she was here, but he sure was glad she'd chosen today for another visit. People filed into the pew behind them, greeting everyone before taking their seats. They all knew Lauren by name, and she chatted pleasantly with adults and children alike. What a difference from the timid woman who'd landed here not long ago. He wondered if she knew just how far she'd come since she'd arrived.

When things settled, he leaned in to murmur, "I talked to my dad this morning."

Her gorgeous eyes sobered immediately, and she frowned. "How did it go?"

"Not well, but it's done." It felt good to tell someone the truth for a change, instead of dodging it. "I told him he has to get his act together by Memorial Day, 'cause I'm taking that job my buddy offered me in Boston."

"Boston," she echoed with a clear understanding of what that meant for him. "Good for you, finally making it happen. They must have some amazing old buildings there."

"Amazing and falling-down," he joked. "Just my style."

She didn't laugh as he'd anticipated, and he asked, "Something wrong?"

"No. I just… Never mind."

Over the years, Ben had learned that when a woman said "never mind," that was the time to pay attention. "You just what?"

"I thought you'd be staying here for a while, to finish your house and all."

He shrugged. "If it's not done before I go, I'll sell it as-is. I got it for peanuts, so I'll still make some money. That way, the new owners can finish it off however they want."

"Okay."

It was the right response, but her tone sounded off to him, and he puzzled over it while the organist struck the opening chords of "How Great Thou Art." As they stood to sing, an odd question popped into his head.

Was Lauren thinking of staying in Holiday Harbor? If she was, did the idea of him being there have any bearing on her decision? And if the answer to that was yes, how did he feel about it?

After the heart-wrenching confrontation with his father, Ben had gotten his fill of emotional tugs for a while, so he put Lauren out of his mind and focused on hitting all the notes. Music had never been his strength, but it was a lot easier than anything else he'd dealt with today.

"So whattya think?"

Crossing his arms on the counter at Toyland, Ben's face was a picture of enthusiasm. Unfortunately, he'd lost Lauren somewhere between Center of Vision and Horizon Line, and she'd ceased to follow anything he was saying. Then again, it was Friday afternoon, and she might just be tired from another challenging week of learning the ropes. "What will it look like?"

"Like this," he replied, pushing the architectural-style drawing closer as if that would help. "I did it from a kid's perspective to give you a better idea how it'll function. It's pretty much what we discussed the other day when I came in to take measurements."

Deciding it was time to come clean, she laughed. "I'll have to take your word on that. I was expecting a more detailed version of the sketch you did at dinner, not a bunch of lines with dimensions and squiggly marks."

"Those are for the pivoting door," he clarified with a grin. "Sorry about that. Sometimes I get carried away with what I'm doing and forget most folks need pictures instead of blueprints. Come on, and I'll show you what I have in mind."

As they went into the far back corner that had been set aside for the new project, she asked, "Those plans really make sense to you?" When he nodded, her admiration of his skill went up several notches. "Did you go to architectural school?"

"Nope."

"How did you learn so much on your own?"

"Here and there. Workshops, online classes, stuff like that. Why?"

He was a lot smarter than she'd given him credit for, but she'd never tell him so. First, it was the kind of backhanded compliment she'd gotten enough times to avoid giving them. Second, it would lead her dangerously close to other personal observations she'd rather keep to herself. She and Ben were doing well as friends whose paths would soon head off in very different directions. Saying or doing anything that might alter that would not only be foolish, it could end up being hurtful.

When they paused in the area taped off for the Playtime zone, she said, "I'm impressed. I was in college for four years and didn't learn even half as much as you did all by yourself."

Cocking his head in the inquisitive gesture she'd come to realize was part of his personality, he grinned. "You probably learned more than you think. The trick is to use what you know and add to it as you go along. Keeps life interesting."

"I guess."

"Like what you're doing here," he continued in an encouraging tone. "You're not just filling in for Julia while she's— Where is she again?"

"Floral emergency."

"Right. While she's at the florist, you're filling out an order for building blocks, helping customers and working on a new idea with me. To me, that's incredible. I'm not an idiot, but I can only do one thing at a time."

"Thanks. It's called multitasking." It wasn't a grand compliment, but she knew he meant it, and his praise made her stand up a little straighter. Pride, she realized with a start. She hadn't experienced that emotion in so long she'd almost forgotten what it felt like. "Okay, now show me what you're talking about."

"Over here—" he went to the back wall and spread his arms wide "—we've got the big, fancy wardrobe for all the gear you and your fellow princesses will need."

The way he referred to her as a princess made her want to giggle, but she put a firm stop to that to avoid sounding like a teenager with a crush. "Gear? They're not mountain climbers, y'know."

"Whatever. Anyway, it looks like it's free-standing, but it's not. I'll build it out with storage behind doors on both sides, and in the center, there's this gigantic mirror." Pausing, he held up a finger with a mischievous grin. "Only it's not just a mirror. The whole thing pivots around a center pole, and on the other side is a rack with rows of angled shelves that have lips on the front. They'll be all different sizes, to hold the construction vehicles and sandbox toys."

Lauren sighed. "Shelves with lips? Are you serious?"

"Well, yeah." He obviously had no clue why she was so confused, but he took a moment to come up with a better explanation. Chuckling, he said, "Like at a shoe store."

His humor was contagious, and she laughed. "Okay, now *that* I understand."

While he outlined his concept for a sandbox with a clamp-down cover that would form a stage floor, she marveled at the creative way his mind worked. When he was finished, she commented, "This is great, Ben. I'm really impressed."

"Thanks, but they're your ideas."

"Maybe, but you made them work." That didn't seem like enough, so she added, "I guess we make a good team."

A lazy grin slowly spread across his face, and his eyes twinkled in approval. "Yeah, we do. That reminds me, do you have a date for Nick and Julia's wedding?"

Her foolish heart tripped over itself, and she headed back to the counter to give herself a few moments to get it back under control. "No. Why?"

"I was wondering if you'd like to go with me."

Yes! she wanted to shout, but she caught herself just in time. While they'd never discussed it openly, it was clear neither of them was looking for a relationship right now. If she freaked over his totally platonic invitation to their friends' wedding, he might get the wrong idea about her. Hoping she appeared cool and composed, she glanced at the computer screen for nonexistent email and nodded.

"Sure. That way we won't get stuck being seated at the singles-only table." His clueless expression made her laugh. "Don't tell me you've never gone to a wedding stag."

"Okay, I won't."

He punctuated that with a playful smirk, and she rolled her eyes. "You're hopeless. What am I gonna do with you? Never mind," she quickly added. "Don't answer that."

With yet another irresistible grin, he pushed away from the counter and sauntered out the door. She was trying not to fall for his small-town boy routine, but he wasn't making it easy on her. Fortunately, their lives were on parallel tracks, and in another month, Ben Thomas would be one of the many pleasant memories she'd treasure from her stay in Holiday Harbor.

"I know that look," Julia commented as the bells over the door announced her return. "What's going on?"

Lauren deftly slid a spreadsheet printout over Ben's sketches. Julia had put her in charge of the Playtime project, insisting she trusted her implicitly. Lauren wanted her friend to be surprised when she saw the final product. "Nothing. Is everything all right with the florist?"

"Almost. Evidently, she has a new assistant who heard me say *gardenias* but wrote down *zinnias*."

"You're kidding. I've never seen those at a wedding."

"My point exactly." Her brow furrowed in exasperation, Julia sighed. "We still have two more weeks to go. I'm not sure I'll make it."

"Your mom will be here next week," Lauren pointed out. "She'll take care of everything after that, and you can relax and do the pampered-bride thing."

At the mention of her mother, Julia's strained expression eased into a smile. "That sounds wonderful. By the way, this morning she told me she wants to get all the ladies together for dinner at the French café that just opened over in Oakbridge. You're first on her list, of course."

Gisele Stanton had a knack for making sure things got done the right way, Lauren recalled fondly. While Julia had flatly refused a typical shower, the mother of the bride wasn't going to let that stop her from celebrating her daughter's upcoming marriage in style. "Sounds great. When?"

"Next Saturday, at seven. No gift," she insisted with a hand in the air to stall any protest Lauren might make. "Just yourself. Bree and Lainie will be there, along with Mavis, Ann, Amelia and a few others. I made Mom promise to keep it under a dozen."

Not very likely, Lauren thought but kept the comment to herself. Unlike Julia, Gisele's normal mode of operation was filled with grand gestures rather than small ceremonies. That the wedding video wouldn't be beamed to the Stantons' many acquaintances around the world was a major concession for the very sociable ambassador's wife.

"I'll be there," Lauren agreed then got back to business. "I sorted out the mix-up with those Easter bunnies, and to make it right, the vendor gave you the correct ones for half price. I added the credit into the bookkeeping entries, so we can charge future orders against it until it's gone."

"Good job. What else did I miss while I was gone?" Once she was up to speed, Julia rewarded Lauren with a proud smile. "You're a real pro now. I won't have to think about Toyland even once while Nick and I are away wherever he's taking me."

"I try." The praise settled nicely, and she returned the smile. "He still won't tell you where you're going?"

"He's determined to surprise me, so I'll just have to wait and see. Since you're doing so well, we can stay a whole month."

While she appeared completely serious, her crystal-blue eyes twinkled merrily, and Lauren laughed. "Don't you dare! I like this place and all, but I'm not planning on making it a full-time thing."

It slipped out before she could stop it, and her friend's expression perked with curiosity. "Does that mean you have something else in mind?"

"Well, not really," she hedged, unwilling to ruin her embryonic plan by saying it out loud. "Just something I've been kicking around."

"I've never heard you mention anything you wanted to do, other than travel."

"Like I said, it's nothing right now."

"If that changes, you'll let me know?" When Lauren nodded, Julia went on. "Good, because I want to be the first to jump in and support you. You've been disappointed a lot in the past, and you deserve to be happy."

As Julia pulled out her ringing cell phone, her words echoed in Lauren's mind with the solid ring of the truth. Much to her surprise, Lauren realized she felt exactly the same way. It was time to put her failures aside and look to the future. The fact that she didn't have all the answers yet didn't intimidate her anymore. And that gave her hope that her difficult past had finally begun to let her go.

When Julia ended her call, she turned to Lauren with the look of a child who'd just been handed her favorite treat. "Can you cover for me a while longer?"

"Sure, but why?"

"That was Nick. The house we want to buy is about to go on the market. If we can get over there now, we can put in a private offer before anyone else even knows it's for sale."

Lauren was thrilled, but she couldn't quite believe their good fortune. "How does he know that?"

"The owners are friends of his, and he's been hounding them for weeks," Julia explained with a quick laugh. "When he wants something, he hammers away from every angle until he gets it."

Her very cultured boss was pretty much bouncing with excitement, and Lauren couldn't keep back a grin. "That must be how he ended up with you."

"More or less," she confirmed on her way out. "I'll be back as soon as I can."

"No rush! We'll celebrate when you get back."

Julia waved in response, and the door jingled its own congratulations as it swung shut behind her. Alone again, Lauren roamed through the shop to make sure everything was neatly put away. When she reached the back corner, she paused near the velvet curtains she and Julia had put up, with a glittery sign hung on a gold cord: *Surprises In Progress—No Peeking.*

Lauren ran a finger through one of the tassels, imagining how everything would look when Ben was finished with his super-secret project. Just beyond the curtain stood the door that led upstairs, and she strolled past it on her way through.

An idea popped up out of nowhere, and she stopped to look back over her shoulder while a plan began spinning in her mind. She had no doubt Nick and Julia would end up with their dream house. When they moved into it, the apartment upstairs would become available. That meant that if someone wanted to make a permanent move to this charming little town, they wouldn't have to hunt very long for a place to live.

And if that someone was her, Lauren mused with a smile, she could make her fresh start right here in Holiday Harbor. Surrounded by good, caring people, with one of her dearest friends only a stone's throw away. She had no doubt Julia would agree to it, or to her staying on as an employee and the coordinator of Playtime.

Working with kids had become the passion she'd been searching for since college, and she couldn't imagine a more perfect scenario for her, both professionally and personally. In fact, the only problem she foresaw was convincing the apartment's very generous owner to set some kind of rent. The more she thought about it, the more the idea appealed to her. She'd come here with no goal beyond escaping her cage in New York, and now she had an honest-to-goodness strategy for moving forward.

It felt fabulous.

The following Monday morning, Ben had mixed emotions while he headed north of town to begin a new roofing job. It was warm for the last week in April, and as he drove along the coast, the sun was just starting to peek over the cliffs. He glanced toward the lighthouse, which was shrouded in pink-tinged fog, waiting for the rising temperature to burn off the mist. It was a beautiful sight, and he understood why so many visitors set their alarms for dawn so they could admire it close-up before the tide swept in and swallowed up the beach.

He was glad Boston had its own harbor, he thought with genuine gratitude. The picture might be a little different, but after growing up surrounded by the moody Atlantic, he had a feeling he'd miss the ocean if he went someplace where he couldn't see it every day.

Once he left the coastline in his rearview mirror, his mind returned to more practical concerns. With the Thomas and Sons trailer bouncing and rattling behind him, he wondered if his father would show up for work today. If he did, Ben wasn't sure how to handle it.

If he didn't—well, Ben had given him fair warning. Sighing in resignation, he sent up a silent prayer for the strength to handle whatever was coming.

When he rounded the bend that led to their customer's home, he saw his father's battered pickup already in the driveway. Breathing a "Thank You, Lord," Ben turned in and parked beside him.

Be cool, he cautioned himself as he stepped out. *Make him think you expected him to be here.* He appeared to be slightly worse for wear, but to Ben's eyes, no sight had ever looked better. "Morning, Dad."

"Morning, son. I made my decision," he added hesitantly.

"I see that. Good for you."

They stood awkwardly at arm's length from one another. Ben wasn't sure what to say or do next, and evidently neither was his father.

"I talked to Pastor McHenry yesterday afternoon," he confided with a grimace. "It was hard, but you were right. He gave me a lot to think about. Reminded me I'm still God's child, and they'll both be there for me if I just ask them for help."

Ben was thrilled to hear that, but he said, "This isn't about me being right. It's about you getting strong enough to deal with Mom leaving so you can move on with your life."

"I didn't want to talk about her," his dad growled, "but the pastor forced me to think back over the years, how tough they were sometimes. Afterward, I realized she left me a long time ago. She just hadn't taken off yet."

Sadly, Ben had experienced that particular epiphany as a teenager, and he had a pretty good idea how much it hurt his father to own up to it. "That's real progress, Dad. I'm proud of you."

Another, more confident smile. "So'm I. I did everything I could to make her happy, but it wasn't enough. That's not my fault, or even hers. It just is."

That didn't strike Ben as something the pastor would say, and he cocked his head with a grin. "That sounds like Amelia Landry talking."

"Yeah." Dragging out the word, his father rubbed the back of his neck like a sheepish teenager confessing a crush. "She came over to check on me, and we talked about it for a while. She's kinda loony, but that woman has a lot more sense than folks give her credit for."

Delivered with fondness, the compliment spoke volumes about how far his father had come in a few short days. Figuring it was time to build on that, Ben suggested, "They're calling for rain day after tomorrow. How 'bout we set a new record in roofing?"

"Sounds good to me. One more thing, though." Fishing in his pocket, he pulled out a silver coin. On the front was a pyramid with Recovery and 24 Hours engraved on it, along with some other inspiring words. Ben flipped it over to find the Serenity Prayer, asking God for help in changing what we can and accepting the things we can't. He knew a few people who had these, and he recognized it immediately. Stunned beyond words, he regarded his staunchly independent father with newfound respect. "You went to an A.A. meeting?"

"It was Amelia's idea, and at first I didn't think it'd work for me. But she dragged me there and sat with me so I wouldn't bolt. Some of the folks there used to be way worse off than me, and hearing them made me believe I can be the kind of man I used to be." Pausing, he rested a hand on Ben's shoulder. "The kind who runs his own business, instead of letting his son work himself half to death to keep things going. You stepped up when I needed you, but I can take it from here."

In that moment, everything Ben had done over the past several months was suddenly worthwhile. The long talks he'd begun to assume had amounted to nothing suddenly had value, and the gratitude shining in his father's eyes was all the reward Ben needed. He couldn't talk around the lump in his throat, and gladly went into his dad's open arms for a fierce hug.

"I love you, son," he murmured in a watery voice. Holding him away for a long look, he added, "You've got real talent, and it's wasted on the projects we get around here. I know you're gonna do a bang-up job in Boston with Davy."

Totally stunned, Ben couldn't believe what he'd just heard. But the confident gaze never wavered, telling him this was truly what Dad wanted for him. Still, their recent history was fresh in his mind, and he wisely hedged. "He won't need me till June. In the meantime, I'll keep on with you, if that's okay."

"Fair enough, but end of May I'll be helping you pack for your trip."

"Sounds good," Ben agreed with a grin.

"For now, we should go warn these poor people it's about to get pretty loud."

They both laughed and headed inside as if they'd never had a care in the world. Still uneasy, Ben hoped the upward spiral would keep going. He'd had enough of the downward one to last him the rest of his life.

Chapter Eight

"Bowling? Nick said they're going bowling?"

Laden with sarcasm, the question came from Bree Landry, who sat in the backseat of Julia's car. A petite woman with auburn hair and dark, intelligent eyes, Lauren had connected with her when she stopped in to visit Julia on her way to her husband Cooper's law office. The three of them had ended up chatting like long-lost sorority sisters, and Lauren had learned more about Cooper, Nick and Ben than she technically needed to know.

"That's what he said," Julia confirmed. "Why?"

"You know why," Bree scoffed. "When Nick's involved, you never know what's *really* going on."

"His brother-in-law, Todd Martin, is the best man, so he's in charge of the bachelor party,"

Julia reasoned. "I'm sure he'll keep things mostly under control."

"Todd will," Lauren agreed, "but will the rest of them go along? When Ben gets something in his head, there's no talking him out of it."

It was suddenly so quiet in that car, the chorus of some oldie's pop song came through the speakers loud and clear. Bree and Julia traded a look in the rearview mirror, and Lauren realized they might misinterpret her comment. "It's such a pain," she added in hopes of diverting any big—and incorrect—romantic ideas they might be spinning.

Fortunately, Bree let her off the hook. "Tell me about it. I love Cooper, but sometimes he drives me completely bonkers. Like this past weekend…"

She went on to describe his latest project at their house, and Lauren let out a relieved sigh. She'd have to be more careful about discussing Ben, she cautioned herself. If she didn't watch what she said, people were going to get the wrong idea about the two of them.

When they arrived at the café, a silver stretch limo was parked beside the curb. Tiny white twinkle lights adorned the slender trees out front, and the deep-set mullioned windows were hung with ivy and roses twined with more lights. Small tables and chairs stood on the sidewalk, and Lauren's mind flashed back to the darling bistros she and Julia had visited in Paris. Gisele couldn't have found a more perfect spot for this evening if she'd tried, and Lauren was certain she'd tried very, very hard.

There wasn't another car in sight, and as the girls stepped out, Lauren grinned at Julia. "Looks like your mom's here."

"She hired the limo to pick up Ann, Lainie and the others in style." Giggling, she said, "I can just imagine the look on Mavis's face when this monster showed up at the lighthouse."

Laughing, the three of them entered the restaurant. It wasn't very big, and a quick glance around showed Lauren it was completely empty except for a large round table in the center of the room. The sound of a joke told in a French accent reached them at the door, and they followed the sound of laughter to where the party had already begun.

"Ma pétite!" Gisele exclaimed, rushing to hug Julia as if she hadn't seen her earlier that day. In a blink, she reached out to embrace Bree and Lauren, giving each of them a two-cheek kiss. Stepping back, she motioned with a graceful wave. "Please, join us. Now that we're all here, the fun can start."

Julia let out a mock groan. "What did you do? I asked you to keep things simple."

"I did," she insisted with an Oscar-winning look of complete innocence. "I invited only your closest friends for a wonderful meal. How is that complicated?"

"And what else?" When Gisele merely smiled, Julia shook her head and opened her menu.

Lauren couldn't believe her friend had given up so easily. Apparently, she was more concerned about this setup than the bride was. Leaning in, she whispered, "Why did she close down the restaurant?"

"I guess we'll find out later."

Chuckling, Bree said, "Your mom reminds me of Amelia. A big heart and full of surprises."

The two women in question had their heads together over the dessert menu, discussing which they wanted to try so they'd know how much of an entrée they should order. Munching on fresh bread and salads, they chatted about the wedding and easily settled into a rhythm of group discussion and whispered comments to each other. When the chef came out to check on them, the usually gruff Mavis charmed him by proclaiming his escargots the "best little garden critters I ever ate."

Gisele's surprise turned out to be a small jazz combo who not only knew Gershwin and Ellington but also an impressive array of pop and classic rock songs. Once they'd finished dessert, their hostess nodded to the conductor, who cued the band for some kind of jive. Clearly delighted with his choice, Gisele jumped up and urged everyone to dance.

"I won't forget that anytime soon," Bree murmured, nodding to where Chef Henri was jitterbugging with Mavis. Holding her phone at a discreet height, she winked at Lauren and hit the record button.

Lauren appreciated being included in the joke, and she laughed. "You'd better not let her find out you have that. She'd kill you."

Clearly unfazed, Bree linked arms with Lauren and Julia, steering them out to the dance floor. "Come on, girls. If Mavis can do this, so can we."

Now it made sense that Gisele had chosen to empty the place, Lauren thought, while they joined the dancing. None of them would have done this in front of strangers, but since it was just them, no one felt too self-conscious to let go and enjoy themselves. Lainie was sandwiched between her mother and Amelia, trying to learn the steps while all three of them laughed nonstop at her efforts. Finally, she gave up and settled for shuffling along to the beat.

Surrounded by lighthearted people and beautiful French artwork, Lauren was struck by a sudden realization.

These women were her friends. In a few short weeks, she'd made more of them than she had in nearly a year in New York. Not by impressing them with her wit or blinding them with her looks, but simply by being herself.

And tonight was only the beginning, she reminded herself. The wedding was next weekend, and then Julia would be gone for however long her secret honeymoon lasted. That meant Lauren would be on her own in Holiday Harbor for the first time. Not long ago, just the thought of it would have filled her with dread.

Now she was pleased to find she was actually looking forward to it.

The day of Nick and Julia's wedding couldn't have been more perfect.

Lauren sat on the aisle so she had an unobstructed view for herself and the pictures she was snapping about every thirty seconds. With her father's guidance, she'd splurged on a jazzy 35mm digital camera, and she planned to get the most out of it. When the organist switched over from background music to one of Mozart's more uplifting melodies, everyone turned toward the open double doors expectantly. Mindless of etiquette, Lauren stepped into the center of the chapel to get a clear shot of Hannah Martin and her basket of rose petals.

Dressed in pink organza with a garland of delicate roses and baby's breath in her hair, she resembled a life-size china doll. No skipping today, Lauren noted while she snapped frame after frame of the flower girl's dignified march toward the altar. When she was close to her father, Todd, he reached over to hug her and pointed Hannah to her spot as Lainie came down the aisle behind her. Ben was holding baby Noah, who chirped his approval of the opening act.

The organist, who had the timing of a real pro, waited for the laughter to die down before starting the wedding march. While everyone else stood and watched the doorway, Lauren took the opportunity to focus her lens on Nick. Standing there in his black tuxedo with his hands folded in front of him, he was the picture of decorum.

The moment he saw Julia, his expression softened into a smile full of love and admiration for the woman he was about to marry. Lauren's eyes welled with delighted tears, and she blinked them away while she stepped out of the aisle to give Julia and her father a clear path.

The bride's innate sense of understated style came through in the elegant sheath gown and fingertip veil that suited her so perfectly that Gisele had broken down in tears when she saw it. Pausing by her mother, Julia leaned in for a quick hug, murmuring something that made Gisele beam with pride. And with all she must have on her mind today, as she passed the front pew, Julia smiled at Lauren and Ben, reaching in to tap Noah playfully on the nose.

It was a lovely, generous thing to do, and Lauren knew she'd remember it forever.

Now that she felt at home in Holiday Harbor, it was wonderful to sit up front in the Safe Harbor Church, misty-eyed while the smiling couple repeated their vows in front of God and the congregation.

When they were finished, Pastor McHenry embraced them together and looked out into the chapel with a joyful smile. "And now, it's with great pride that I present to you, Mr. and Mrs. Nick McHenry."

The organist launched into something joyful, and everyone stood up, cheering and applauding. Since the weather had cooperated so nicely, the reception was set up out in the square, so no one had to rush off anywhere. Including the newlyweds, Lauren noted with curiosity.

Instead of hurrying away as people normally did, they stayed in the church, talking with their guests as they made their way toward the doors at a leisurely pace. So rather than running the gauntlet of a receiving line, they casually blended in with the crowd headed outside.

While they waited for things to thin out a little, Ben lifted Noah to his shoulders so he could get a better view. "Great wedding, huh?"

"Just like she wanted," Lauren agreed. "I'm so happy for them both."

"Yeah, me, too. They're quite the pair."

She caught a hint of sadness in his tone, and knew he was thinking about the end of his parents' marriage. It was only natural, she supposed, but she didn't want it to put a blemish on what should be a day filled with happiness. While they merged in with the other retreating guests, she asked, "Do you know what Nick has planned for their honeymoon? It's been driving Julia bonkers."

Grinning, Ben shook his head. "Far as I know, he didn't tell a soul. All I know is he booked it through a travel agent way outta town so no one would get wind of what he did. Said Julia surprises him all the time, and he wanted to do the same for her."

Although she'd gotten to know him fairly well, it still astonished Lauren that the dark, intense editor had such a soft heart. "That's really sweet. It's still making her crazy, though."

"Not for much longer," Ben assured her as they went down the steps and headed for the square. "He's gonna announce it first thing before folks get distracted by the food."

"Smart man."

Laughing, they both turned toward the booming sound of Pastor McHenry's voice calling everyone to the gazebo. Draped in ropes of the gardenias Julia had fought to have delivered in time, it was set up for the wedding party, who filed into their spots. Offering his hand to Julia, Nick escorted her to their seats but motioned for her to remain standing.

Reaching beneath the table, he lifted out a stack of three boxes wrapped in white tulle and topped with bouquets of multicolored roses. The wrapping was so gorgeous that Lauren couldn't begin to imagine what might be inside.

"I know you're all dying to dig into the buffet, so I'll get right to it. Most of you know my wife—" a smile for Julia "—is the owner of Toyland here in town. With that in mind, I borrowed a few things for today."

"Did you know about that?" Ben whispered.

"No, and by the shocked looks they're giving me, her assistants didn't know, either."

"He's good."

He was something, anyway, but Lauren put that aside as Nick handed Julia the top box. Judging by the look on her face when she opened it, she had no idea what to think of the toy train she pulled out. "I'm lost."

"Try the next one," he suggested, eyes twinkling in fun.

The next box held a toy boat, which didn't clear things up at all. The final—and largest—one yielded a stuffed husky dog. All the items were from the shelves at Toyland, and while Lauren recognized them instantly, she had no idea what they had to do with their honeymoon.

"When you marry the daughter of a U.S. Ambassador—" Nick nodded to the Stantons "—it's tough to book a trip to somewhere she's never been. Thanks to Julia's parents, though, I finally came up with a place."

"Alaska," she breathed, her eyes shining with excitement. When he nodded, she threw her arms around him in a joyful hug, kissing him soundly while everyone whooped and applauded.

"We take the train across Canada—" Nick set it on the table. "Then board a ship—" he set that beside the train "—for our cruise into Glacier Bay and up the coast, where we'll meet up with a dogsled team for our trip into Denali."

Lauren had known Julia for almost ten years and had never seen her at a loss for words. But after that breathless squeak, it seemed all she could do was smile and shake her head in disbelief. She whispered something to Nick, who laughed and put a steadying arm around her waist.

"Okay, that's it," he announced. "Let's eat!"

Somehow, Ben managed to balance a sleeping Noah against his chest with one hand and load up a plate with the other. While watching him deftly juggle the two, Lauren got a glimpse of what he'd be like with his own kids someday. A solid, dependable father, attentive and endlessly patient.

Much like he was with her.

The revelation struck Lauren with a force that almost knocked her back a step. Her powerful reaction was silly, of course, and she brushed it off as she chose her own meal from among the delectable-smelling comfort foods stocking the buffet. While they ate and chatted quietly to avoid waking Noah, that feeling receded but never really went away. Was she starting to fall for Ben? she wondered with real concern. They'd been spending a lot of time together working on the new area for Toyland, so it was a definite possibility. In truth, during their design sessions and not so strictly business dinners, she'd gotten to know him better than a lot of the men she'd actually dated.

Before she could make up her mind, Todd stopped by their table to get his son.

"Thanks a lot, Ben," he whispered, settling Noah's cheek on his shoulder. "I can take it from here."

"No problem. He's a real trouper. And drooler," he added, chuckling as he wiped his damp tie with his napkin.

Todd's grin clearly said he'd experienced the same thing more than once. "Sorry about that."

"Not a big deal. Just gives me an excuse to do this." In one swift motion, Ben unhitched the tie and slung it over the back of his chair. After opening the top button of his shirt, he slumped in his chair and sighed. "Much better."

Todd thanked him again then left them alone at their table. Leaning back, Ben crossed his long legs in front of him and looked over at her. Crazy as it was, Lauren felt like he was studying her, trying to decide something important.

"What?" she asked.

"Y'know, I think I forgot to tell you how amazing you look. Blue is definitely your color."

She felt a blush creeping up her cheeks, which was totally unlike her. Staring into her closet that morning, something had prompted her to choose the same dress she'd been wearing when he referred to her as "sunshine." Now that he'd noticed it—and complimented her so nicely—she wondered if subconsciously she'd picked this one hoping for just that response.

Still, her reaction was absurd. It wasn't the first time a man had flattered her, after all. There was absolutely no reason to behave like a shy teenager at her first dance. Except that this time, the approval came from Ben, a sweet, simple guy who said what he meant and meant what he said. Unlike Jeremy, he didn't use flattery to manipulate people, or to twist the truth around in an attempt to convince them he was right and they were wrong.

This man lounging in a chair at a formal event believed she looked amazing, and she rewarded him with her brightest smile. "Thank you. You clean up pretty well, too."

"Don't get used to it," he said with a grin. Standing, he held out a hand. "But since we both look so good, maybe we should go dance."

He didn't have to ask her twice. Lauren had been dying to try out some of the ballroom moves she'd watched Nick and Julia practicing the past couple of weeks. "I'd love to."

Ben rested his hand lightly on her back and led her over to the parquet dance floor the band had laid out. Just as they got there, the upbeat tempo shifted down to something more sedate, and he paused at the edge of the floor.

Raising a questioning eyebrow, he asked, "Are you okay with a slow one?"

Her heart kicked with anticipation, but she covered her bizarre response with a shrug. "Sure, if you are."

"A waltz with the prettiest lady here?" he teased, his eyes twinkling with male admiration. "Try and stop me."

As he took her in his arms and started them off, she gazed up at him in total disbelief. When she landed in Holiday Harbor, she was literally running for her life, too frightened to go back and terrified of what the future might hold for her. But now, surrounded by caring people and wrapped up in Ben's strong, capable arms, she felt completely and utterly safe.

It was a wonderful feeling.

Holding Lauren in his arms was the most incredible thing Ben had ever done.

She was just the right height for him to rest his cheek in her hair while they danced, and it took everything he had not to do it. But that would be way too intimate a gesture for two people who'd agreed—more than once—to be friends. Unfortunately, the temptation was growing by the second, and he breathed a sigh of relief when the band switched to a quicker song.

Putting an extra step of distance between them, he met those brilliant blue eyes and actually forgot what he was going to say. Deciding it was best to keep things light, he said, "I think I forgot to thank you for being my wedding date. Folks might stare if I was dancing out here all by myself."

"Like that would ever happen," she scoffed. "More likely, all the single girls would be lined up, pushing and shoving to see who could get to you first."

Her comment didn't sound even remotely romantic, and Ben congratulated himself on avoiding a potentially awkward situation with her. The problem was, he had no trouble imagining it going differently, with her gazing up at him while he leaned in to kiss her.

"Hi, kids," Amelia greeted them, smiling as she danced over with his father. "Having fun?"

"Absolutely," Lauren assured her as they sailed off into the crowd. Smiling herself, she added, "Your dad looks like he's having a good time."

"He and Amelia have been friends since they were kids," Ben replied. "She's been spending a lot of time with him lately, and I think it's really helping."

"It can be tough to handle everything on your own."

Her tone was laced with empathy, and he realized she understood loneliness better than most. Isolated from friends and family by a controlling egomaniac, things must have gotten pretty awful for her. Wanting to reassure her, he tipped her chin up with his finger so she was looking directly at him. "As long as you're here, you won't have to manage everything by yourself ever again."

"I know. Leave the hard stuff up to God."

That wasn't exactly what he meant, but he wasn't sure how to explain himself without giving her the wrong idea about his feelings for her, so he changed the subject. "How're things at Nick and Julia's house? I haven't seen it since I hauled that humongous dollhouse of hers over there for them."

"It's a little disorganized, but everything's there now. Since the sellers agreed to let them rent it until the closing, we've been packing up her stuff. The last box went out yesterday, so everything's set up for when they get back. She's really excited, and I'm thrilled for them."

Glancing around, she edged in an extra step that put them much closer than was strictly necessary. While it wasn't all that comfortable for him, Ben felt honored to be the one she trusted enough to allow him so close. "Can you keep a secret?"

Judging by the delighted sparkle in her eyes, it was something big, and again he was touched by the faith this cynical city girl had in him. "Uh-huh."

"I'm staying here in Holiday Harbor. Julia said I can live above Toyland and work there while I get my own business started." Taking a breath, she rushed ahead. "I was looking around during one of my walks, wondering what kind of store I could open. One day, it hit me—there's no day care in town."

"There was once, in that closed-down storefront across from the bank. Then the economy took a hit, and they had to close down."

"That's what Ann told me, and it got me thinking. I love the kids who come into the store, and a lot of them are either preschoolers or in kindergarten. If parents had an affordable place for them to be, even part-time, that would be good, right?"

"Very good," he answered without hesitation. "Dependable kid care is tough to find around here."

"I even came up with a name," she confided with an adorable giggle. "Jumping Beans."

"That's perfect."

Not girlie or boyish, but an apt description of the kids who'd go there for a fun morning or all day with Lauren. He easily pictured her not only succeeding but loving her job. While she excitedly described how she'd set up her playroom and arts-and-crafts area, Ben did his best to keep a smile plastered on his face. Because as wonderful as it all sounded, for some reason his heart was rapidly sinking in his chest.

He should be psyched for her, he scolded himself. Any other day, he would have been, so what was different today? At the wedding of two of his closest friends, dancing with the prettiest guest there, he should be enjoying it all without a second thought.

Good things were happening with him, too,

he realized, and when she was finished, he said, "I've got some news myself."

"Really? What?"

"I officially signed on for that restoration job in Boston. I'm heading down there June 1."

Gasping, Lauren launched herself at him in an exuberant hug that nearly knocked him over. When she stepped back, he noticed she didn't even try to slip from his loose embrace. Was she aware of that, or was she just so caught up in the moment she hadn't noticed?

"That's awesome!" she approved, eyes shining with delight. "Congratulations."

"Thanks."

"Isn't it great?" she gushed. "Both of us are getting a chance to make our dreams come true."

It was great, Ben agreed silently. He just couldn't figure out why she seemed more enthusiastic about his new position than he was. While he was trying to work his way through his suddenly baffling emotions, a white stretch limo floated up the street and parked not far from the dance floor.

When the driver got out and opened one of the rear doors, the band conductor turned to the crowd and held up his hands. "Ladies and gentlemen, the bride and groom will be leaving shortly. If you'd like to wish them well, please head over to the far side of the green."

Laughing and talking all at once, everyone followed his directions, trailing after Nick and Julia like a warmhearted gaggle of geese. After hugs for their families, the couple waved goodbye and settled into the elegant car for their ride to the airport in Rockland.

And just like that, another of Ben's childhood friends drove off a married man. It hadn't struck him until just now, but he was the last of the three of them who was still single. Oh, there were still guys in town he'd gone to school with who were bachelors, but Cooper and Nick were the ones who'd always mattered the most to him. Not long ago, Ben would've worn his last remaining single status like a badge of honor.

But now, he wasn't so sure it was a good thing.

With the guests of honor gone, the reception lost its luster for Ben, and judging by Lauren's weary expression, she felt the same way.

"I've been up with Julia since five," she confided. "I think I'll call it a day."

"Yeah, me too. I mean, the calling-it-a-day thing," he added, hoping to coax a smile from her. When she grinned, without thinking he said, "Why don't I walk you home?"

"You mean, across the street?"

"Sure."

"I think I can find my way."

Taking that as a hint she wasn't keen on having him for company, he shrugged. "Okay. Have a nice evening, then."

Her rejection of his offer meant nothing, he told himself as he strode toward the church parking lot. She'd had a long day, and she wanted to be alone. No big deal. But he'd enjoyed spending so much time with her, and he'd assumed she felt the same. Now that he knew otherwise, maybe he could shake the peculiar fascination he seemed to have developed for her when he wasn't paying attention.

He was about to climb into his truck when he heard someone calling his name. Instinctively, he looked over at Toyland, where Lauren was standing on the sidewalk, arms folded in obvious irritation. As he trotted over, it became apparent what the problem was.

Holding up a tiny bag hardly big enough for lip gloss, she shook it in disgust. "I forgot my key. Do you still have the spare Julia gave you when you were rehabbing this place?"

"Sorry." Grimacing, he tried to hold her gaze without flinching, but after several seconds, he couldn't keep it up and had to laugh.

He pulled out his fob and found the door key, unlocking and opening it for her with a bow.

"Oh, you're hilarious." Mad as she sounded, her eyes were dancing with humor. "What am I going to do with you?"

Then she laughed, and suddenly Ben wasn't so anxious to get home. "Since I'm here, could I get a glass of water?"

"Sure, but I'll warn you, it's a disaster upstairs. There are flowers and bits of girl stuff everywhere."

"I don't mind," he assured her smoothly, because it was the truth. Now that Boston was an imminent thing, he wanted to spend every minute he could with her before he left.

At the top of the stairs, she paused for a moment, and he knew she was waiting for Shakespeare's customary greeting. When her eyes drifted toward the now-empty bay window, she frowned. "I forgot Liam came to get him this morning. We were so crazed getting ready, I never got to say goodbye."

Her chin trembled, then firmed quickly, as if she was trying very hard to contain her emotions. Then Ben understood, and he gently said, "You're not just talking about the parrot, are you?"

"I'm so happy for Julia," Lauren confessed in a watery voice. "She loves Nick, and more than anyone I know she deserves to be happy. In her new house, with her new husband, making memories and a family. That's all she's ever really wanted."

The rambling trailed off into tears, and Ben instinctively took her in his arms. Even though she didn't come out and say it, he recognized that those things were all Lauren wanted, too. Like him, her problem was she didn't know how to get them.

He had no clue what to say, so he went with the truth. "I know what you mean. Things change when your friends get married, and I'm gonna miss 'em, too."

"All my friends from high school and college are married," she whimpered into his chest. "What on earth is wrong with me?"

Hearing the desperation in her tone just about broke Ben's lethally soft heart. Stepping back, he gently took her face in his hands. "Lauren, listen to me." Waiting for her to look up at him, he continued. "You're an amazing woman, inside and out. Any guy who doesn't see that isn't worth having."

"You really believe that?"

"I really do."

Smiling, he gently whisked the last of her tears away with the pads of his thumbs. Lashes still damp with sadness, she gazed up at him with so much trust in her eyes, it caught him by surprise.

And it made him want to take her in his arms for a more-than-friends kind of kiss.

The urge was so strong it took everything he had not to give in to the temptation. Instead, he dropped his hands and smoothly pivoted away from her to look around. "Tell you what. Why don't I stay and help you clean up? Then we can set up the furniture the way you want, so the place feels more like yours."

"You don't have to," she hedged, waving away his offer. "I can manage."

While he respected her independent spirit, he couldn't leave her there alone when she'd been in tears only minutes ago. Once he was satisfied she was feeling better, he'd be more than happy to go. Well, mostly. "It'll go faster with more hands."

"Okay, thanks."

Kicking off her shoes, she went into the kitchen to get a couple of garbage bags and a broom. Once the floors were clear of wedding bits, she faced the huge window with its spectacular view of the town below. "Maybe the love seat could go in there. It would make a nice place to sit and read."

"Gotcha."

Ben grabbed one end of it while she picked

up the other, and they slid it into place, adding a side table for good measure. When they'd spun and repositioned the other pieces Julia had left behind, the space felt much cozier. There wasn't much they could do about the tall built-in bookshelves, though, and Lauren frowned at them. "I don't have anything to fill those, so I guess they'll have to stay that way."

"Maybe now that you're staying here, you'll find something to collect."

Turning, she gave him a curious look. "Like what?"

"I don't know," he admitted with a chuckle. "Books, antique gewgaws, china cows. You could print out and frame some of those pictures you've been taking and put 'em in there."

That got her attention, and her face lit up with enthusiasm. "That's a great idea! But I don't want just any frames—they need to be special."

Ben had a pretty good idea where she was headed, but he decided it was more fun to play dumb. "Whattya mean?"

"I mean, I want them to be custom-made. By you."

"I don't know," he stalled with a mock frown. "I don't usually mess with small, fussy stuff like that."

"I'll pay you, if that's what you're after."

Always the city girl, he mused with a grin. "I'm after something more important than money."

Her eyes narrowed suspiciously. "Like what?"

"An extra set of hands. My to-do list is as long as my arm, and if I'm taking on something else, I'm gonna need some help."

Clearly stunned, she blinked at him. "Are you serious?"

"Yes, ma'am. I'll build you as many frames as you think you'll need, then you can come over to my place and stain them however you want."

Judging by the look on her face, that was the last thing she'd expected to hear. She was used to men who took what they wanted, regardless of her wishes, and it had made her distrustful of the male species in general. Before he left for Boston, Ben was determined to convince her that some guys were worth taking a chance on. If she couldn't learn to believe that, she'd never have the life she wanted so desperately.

Finally, she seemed to make up her mind and smiled. "Fine. I'll come over and make frames with you. When?"

"Next week sometime. Just let me know how many you need and when you're coming so I can have everything ready." He decided he'd pushed her far enough for one afternoon and leaned in to kiss her—on the cheek this time. "Have a good night, Lauren."

"You, too. Ben?" When he turned back, she gave him a warm, grateful smile. "Thanks for coming up here with me so I wouldn't be alone the first time. It was really sweet of you."

He felt an offer to stay longer bubbling up from somewhere and gulped it down to keep from making a fool of himself. With a quick wave, he trotted down the stairs before he could blurt out something they'd both regret.

Chapter Nine

Saturday afternoon, Lauren closed up Toyland at five and headed over to Ben's. When she got there, she found him in his garage workshop with the front door wide open to the cool breeze blowing in off the ocean. From inside drifted some classic rock song, and she heard him singing along as if the entire neighborhood couldn't hear him.

He had a decent voice, she decided with a grin, but the air guitar sealed it for her. When the song was finished, she walked in applauding. "Very nice."

"Thanks." He flashed her one of those devastating grins and motioned to the stack of frames on his work bench. "There's a dozen ready to go, sized just the way you wanted."

She'd expected some basic frames, but he'd dressed them up with hand carving and other details that made each one distinctive from the others. Touched by the effort he'd put into them, she said, "These must have taken forever. With all the projects you've got going right now, where did you find the time?"

"Here and there." When she tipped her head in disbelief, he laughed. "Okay, you got me. I figured I'll never finish the house before I leave for Boston, so I quit trying. It freed me up to do a little woodworking."

"I guess so," she commented while she assessed the cans of stain on a nearby shelf. "Does that mean you're going to sell the house as is?"

"Haven't decided yet."

That was news to her, and she stared at him in astonishment. "You're thinking of keeping it? Why?"

He shrugged, and something in his eyes made her heart skip with excitement. Was he considering staying in Holiday Harbor? And if he was, did her putting roots down here have anything to do with his sudden change of heart?

Of course, she'd never ask him that directly. It would sound conceited, and certainly not friend-ish. So she set about satisfying her curiosity in a more roundabout way. Prying open a can of cherry stain to stir it, she casually said,

"After all the effort you've put in here, I guess it's hard to think about giving it up."

"Yeah, it is."

The gentle tone surprised her, and she glanced over to find him staring at her with a pensive expression. Something told her he wasn't referring to the house, and she felt a blush creeping up her cheeks. The problem was, she wasn't really embarrassed. She was pleased. Not terrified, not resistant, but touched. The mere possibility that this solid, stand-up guy could be interested in her made her feel incredible.

Ben had done so much for her, from helping with cookie trays the first day she met him to encouraging her business plans to making frames for her photos. She wished there was some way she could repay some of that kindness. If he decided to stay, she'd have plenty of opportunities, with the added benefit that she'd get to spend more time with the sweetest guy on the planet. Even while her imagination spun through the endless possibilities, she knew they'd never come to be.

She had to let him go. He'd worked hard for years to get this position in Boston, and no matter how much she wanted him to stay with her, she couldn't bring herself to stand in the way of his dreams. They might be happy enough, but for Ben, something would always be missing. He deserved better than that.

While she slathered on stain and rubbed it off the way he'd shown her, Lauren's eyes blurred with tears. When she fled New York for the wilds of northern Maine, she'd never expected to meet someone like Ben. Someone who made her feel safe and cared-for, and no matter how trying her day had been, always found a way to make her smile. She realized she hadn't been saying much, and began searching for a topic that would kick-start a conversation.

While she was struggling with that, a beat-up pickup pulled into the driveway, and Ben angled a look out the door. He was pretty tall, but the man who stepped out of the cab beat him by a good four inches. When Ben's face broke into a huge grin, Lauren instantly knew who his visitor was.

"Eric?"

Dropping the do-hickey he'd been tinkering with, he flew out of the garage and into a bear hug that would have snapped Lauren's spine. When they separated, Ben laughed. "When you left, you said you'd never set foot in this podunk town again. What're you doing here?"

"Dad called. Said you were taking that job in Boston with Davy, so I figured he'd need someone on the crew who's actually swung a hammer a few times." Eric's grayish-blue eyes swung to Lauren with curiosity. "Is this the one everyone's buzzing about?"

"You've still got the manners of a grizzly bear," Ben chided him. "This is Lauren Foster. Lauren, my big brother, Eric."

"Sorry about that. It's been a long day." Offering an apologetic grin, he held out a hand the size of a catcher's mitt. "Pleased to meet you."

"You, too." She'd heard only the barest mention of this guy the whole time she'd been in town, and now she understood why. Rough around the edges didn't begin to describe him, but the gentle way he shook her hand reminded her of Ben.

"I can see you two're busy," he said, "so I'll get going."

"You can crash here if you want," Ben suggested without hesitation. "I've got plenty of room, just not many walls."

"That'd be great. Where do you want me?"

"There's a mostly finished room upstairs next to the bathroom. There's no bed frame, but the mattresses are brand-new. And extralong," he added with a grin.

"For me?" When Ben nodded, Eric returned the smile. "Cool. Thanks."

"Don't mention it."

Eric left the garage and grabbed a single camouflage duffel bag from the front seat of his truck before trudging inside. After the screen door slammed shut behind him, Lauren turned to Ben, whose smile hadn't faded yet. Despite the ribbing, he was obviously thrilled to see his older brother back in town, but she couldn't miss the hint of worry in the weathered lines around his eyes. "Let me guess. Military."

"Army Ranger," he confirmed proudly. "Ten years of combat duty in places I can't even pronounce. He's been out almost a year now, but he's still adjusting."

She couldn't begin to imagine what kind of mental and physical strength Eric must have just to return home in one piece. Many of the men who worked on the force with her father were former soldiers, and she had tremendous respect for them. "He came back here to work with your dad so you could go to Boston without feeling guilty. What a sweet, generous thing to do."

Ben chuckled. "He'd be good with the generous part, but I think it's best not to tell him you think he's sweet. It might go to his head."

Raising a brow, she gave him a little smile. "It hasn't gone to yours. What's your secret?"

"Simple," he retorted with a shameless grin of his own. "I know it's true."

Arrogant, she complained silently as she got back to work, *not to mention cocky.* And despite those less-than-stellar qualities, Ben Thomas still managed to be completely and utterly irresistible. If only they'd met sooner, or if she hadn't been so closed-off for the first month, they might have had something spectacular together.

But he was leaving, and she was staying. No matter what might have been, those were the facts, and she'd have to learn to live with them. And without him.

After a couple of hours, all the frames were stained and varnished and in various stages of drying. Now that Eric was here, Lauren suspected he'd like to spend some time with his brother, so she stretched as if all this brushing and small-talk had worn her out. "That's all I can do for tonight. I think I'll head back to Julia's place."

"It's your place now," he reminded her quickly. "I'd imagine you'll be calling it home before too much longer."

"Probably." It wouldn't feel the same without him around all the time, but she kept that detail to herself. "I really appreciate all your help with this. I'm picking up my photos from the print shop on Monday, and I can't wait to see how they look inside their frames."

"I'll put in the glass and drop 'em by Toyland on Monday."

Such a great guy, she thought for the millionth time. If only she'd figured that out sooner. "Thanks. I guess I'll see you in church tomorrow."

Cocking his head in apparent confusion, he said, "I was planning to walk you back."

"Oh, don't bother. You've got company, and I know the way. Have a good night."

He looked to be on the verge of protesting, so she did the finger-waggling thing and headed out before he had a chance to stop her. She wasn't in a hurry, and she ambled along the sidewalk, stopping to chat with people who called out to her from their porches and front yards. It hadn't taken her long to get used to the Mayberry vibe in this town, she thought with a smile.

When she finally ended up back at Julia's—no, her place—Lauren glanced up at the dark bay window with a frown. Over the past couple of days, she'd become more or less accustomed to having the apartment to herself, but it still echoed with emptiness, as if the building itself was waiting for its owner to return. Lauren cast a long look out toward the harbor, where the last bits of a magnificent sunset were still hanging on.

What a fabulous picture that would make, she thought excitedly. Before the impulse faded, she dashed upstairs for her camera and hurried down to the rocky beach where Ben had begun coaxing her from her self-imposed shell on Easter morning. On her way out to the shore, she caught several shots of the lighthouse framed against an evening sky filled with orange and pink that faded out to deep purple at the edges.

She plunked herself down on that same boulder, snapping frame after frame as the sun gradually slipped over the horizon and out of sight. Leaning back, she looked out on the view she'd grown to value so much. She admired how the ocean was always shifting, never the same one moment to the next. The waves curled relentlessly toward the shore, then back out, engulfing the jagged coastline one minute and then revealing it before rushing in again. Wild and unpredictable, the sea possessed a special kind of beauty even she couldn't describe, however hard she tried. There weren't words for it, or if there were, she hadn't learned them.

After sitting for a while, she found herself wondering what she'd find a little farther up the coast. As she followed the jagged line of rocks, she found a footpath that led alongside the cliffs that vaulted upward from the water's edge. Securing the strap of her camera around her neck, she balanced one hand on the rocky wall and picked her way along, pausing now and then to take another picture.

She glanced back and saw absolutely nothing but raw, rugged coastline. It was as if the town had vanished from the face of the earth, and even the lighthouse resembled a model in the distance. Not long ago, she'd have been terrified to be in this situation, but now she found it exhilarating.

Even though she knew her camera wouldn't capture this untamed scene completely, she kept on snapping pictures, captivated by a world she never knew existed.

The power went out around ten-thirty that night.

A quick look outside showed Ben the entire town was dark, so the wind must have taken down one of the main lines along the highway. Prepared by a lifetime of living through storms, earlier he'd battened down everything outside and had gotten a fire going. With Eric snoring away upstairs, Ben lit the camping lantern sitting on the table and returned to the latest bestselling thriller he'd been trying to find time to read. Written by his favorite author, it had all the twists and turns a mystery fan could ask for.

As an added bonus, it was keeping his mind off Lauren. Well, mostly. He still couldn't shake the impression that she'd wanted to tell him something while they were working on her frames. For some reason, she'd uncharacteristically held back and kept it to herself. She'd tell him when and if she was ready, he reasoned as he settled in and got back to the story. He was in the middle of a spectacular chase scene through the Amazon jungle when it hit him.

Lauren was alone at Toyland.

With no power, she was in the dark in a place she still didn't know all that well. Being a small-town guy, he dealt with this kind of inconvenience all the time, but a lifelong city girl? Probably not.

Picking up his cell phone, he dialed her number and waited for her to answer. Without electricity, the answering machine wouldn't pick up, and he assumed she was feeling her way around the apartment, trying to locate the handset. After a minute, he hung up and tried again. No answer.

Ben's eyes wandered to the French doors,

which framed a good old-fashioned thunderstorm thrashing its way through Holiday Harbor. Waking Eric was never a good idea, so Ben scribbled a note about where he'd gone and left it on the kitchen table.

It didn't normally take long to get downtown, but tonight he had to drive around and over several downed tree limbs and power lines. When he tuned in the weather report, the forecaster was calling it an old-fashioned gale, warning folks to hunker down and stay inside until it was over.

"Good advice," Ben grumbled to himself. As he drove past the double-bay emergency station, he noted that both the fire truck and ambulance were gone. If things got any worse, it would be a long night for them.

At Toyland, he didn't bother knocking but used his key to let himself inside. "Lauren?"

His voice echoed back at him unanswered, and he ran upstairs to check the apartment. Empty. Sheets of rain were battering the bay window, and he heard trees creaking under the force of the howling wind. Out over the harbor, a bolt of lightning flashed through the sky, illuminating the lighthouse in an ominous warning. Ben started counting and got to five, which meant the lightning was five miles out.

He recalled Lauren's comment about loving

storms, and on a hunch, dialed the lighthouse. "Hi, Mavis. This is Ben Thomas. Lauren isn't out there by any chance?"

"Haven't seen her today. Why?"

When he explained, Mavis grumped, "Who's crazy enough to go out in this?"

"I'm thinking maybe the weather was good when she started out but turned bad later on. That can happen pretty fast this time of year."

"On the scanner, I heard the EMT's called out to Schooner Point for a tree that crashed into someone's living room. If she's out in this, we should get a search party together and go find her."

"I hate to roust people for no reason," Ben stalled. "I'm sure she's on her way back."

"What if she tripped and twisted her ankle or something? She could be in trouble with the tide rising, and no one knows where she is."

That was what did it: the thought of Lauren caught out in the madness of an Atlantic storm, drenched and alone. "I'm leaving now. You probably oughta call the sheriff and get things moving."

"Do something for me, boy."

"Yes, ma'am."

"When you find that sweetheart of a girl, tell her she's a stinking moron."

The line clicked off, and despite his serious

errand, Ben had to laugh. Leave it to Mavis to shift from maternal to spitfire in a single breath. Out in his truck, he pulled on a lined fisherman's raincoat, then another over top of it. By the time he found Lauren, she'd welcome something warm and dry to put on.

He stopped at the lighthouse, but Lauren still hadn't shown up there. With the wind shrieking like a banshee and rain driving in sideways, he now shared Mavis's concern. As he set out into the blackness, he reminded himself that Lauren was an intelligent, resourceful woman who certainly had sense enough to find shelter from the rain.

And he knew where she'd go: to the sea caves. She'd been fascinated when he pointed them out to her, and she'd remember him saying some of them were safe at high tide. So he headed down toward the shore, where waves driven by relentless winds smashed into the coast with a vengeance that was awesome to hear.

Deafening, actually, he realized when he shouted her name and his voice slammed back at him in a mouthful of chilling spray. Spitting out the salty water, he paused to wipe his face and tighten the storm flaps on his hood. The rescue cutter was already out in the harbor, sweeping the choppy waves with its searchlight while it plowed through the rough sea. He watched for a few moments, dreading the possibility that they'd come upon Lauren's body floating in the water.

With all the resolve he had, he shook off the morbid thought, knowing it served no purpose other than to slow him down. Lauren was out here somewhere, and like him, his neighbors wouldn't stop hunting until someone found her. As he picked his way down to the narrow strip of beach, Ben sent up a silent prayer for guidance.

If ever there was a time for divine intervention, he figured this was it.

By the time Lauren realized she was trapped, it was too late.

Watching thunderclouds billowing toward shore, she lost sight of anything but the awesome power roiling through them. She strolled along, ignoring everything except the natural display of strength unlike anything she'd ever seen. Nothing but water and wind, she mused, setting her camera to automatically click frame after frame so she could watch. The core of the storm descended so fast, the clouds completely blotted out the moon and every wink of the stars she'd been admiring earlier.

When flashes of lightning began illuminating the multistory waves, she snapped a few more manual pictures and packed up her camera. Since she had no desire to become New England's version of a storm chaser, it was time to go home. She turned to retrace her steps, using the distant lights of the town as a guide. Had she really come that far? she wondered nervously. Not the smartest thing she'd ever done.

Suddenly, everything blinked out, as if some giant hand had flipped a switch and shut off the power. Now, the only light shone from the beacon on the point, and it dawned on her that she was in trouble.

As if that weren't enough, the waves had encroached on the rocky stretch of beach she'd followed to the water's edge, narrowing it to the width of a balance beam. The footing was treacherous, and she stumbled through icy water that tossed her around like a doll. In a desperate attempt to keep her balance, she grabbed for the jagged rocks of the cliff, slicing her hands in the process. One wave was so huge, it swept her off her feet and partway into the surf.

Spitting out brackish water, she decided to find shelter rather than risk having the storm take her out to sea. A slightly blacker opening in the darkness off to her left told her this was one of the caves Ben and Nick had played in when they were kids. As she made her way through the opening, she couldn't see a thing. Waking the view screen of her camera, she swept the faint light around, assessing her options.

It was tiny, but it was dry, and she didn't see any animal nests or droppings. Good. With frigid water lapping at her ankles, she knew she had to make a choice: stay or keep moving. If she settled in here and the tide engulfed her, she'd have to swim out through the churning water and unforgiving rocks. While she was a pretty strong swimmer, she could easily drown. But if she kept going along the shoreline, one misstep would end the same way.

Looking up, she swallowed the fear rising in her throat. "I know You've got a lot going on, but if You've got time, I could really use some help."

Nothing.

She waited a few seconds, but still got no response. Apparently, she was on her own. The next wave soaked her up to her knees, nearly shoving her into the cave against her will. Deciding that was her answer, she sloshed her way toward some rocks that formed a crude set of steps. It wasn't much of a shelter, but she trusted that God had led her here to keep her safe until someone could rescue her.

Using her camera like a flashlight, she carefully climbed the slippery path leading to the kind of shelf Ben had described to her Easter morning. Despite the windbreaker she was wearing, she was soaked. Wrapping her arms around her bent knees, she rocked to keep her shivering muscles from seizing up all together. She might have to make a dash for it on a moment's notice, and everything had to be ready to move. To keep her mind from dwelling on the dire possibilities, she tried singing one of her favorite songs. Against the fury of the storm, her voice sounded small and frightened. That was discouraging, so she stopped.

Desperate for something to do besides shiver and wait, she flipped on her camera screen again and began scrolling through pictures she'd taken during her time in Holiday Harbor. What had begun as a temporary change of venue had turned into quite the adventure, she mused with a grin. From the Easter egg hunt to the changes at Toyland to the tantalizing possibility of starting her own business, she'd gotten much more than she'd bargained for.

When a shot of Ben and her at the wedding flashed onto the screen, she paused. Clucking like the proud father he was, Craig had gotten a shot of them on the outdoor dance floor. Caught up in the fun of the reception, they looked bright and happy in the sunlight.

That was before she knew for certain their paths were headed in different directions, and even now the memory of that conversation made her sad. She wasn't a sentimental person, but she couldn't help touching Ben's face on the little screen. As if his incredible looks weren't enough, he was also the kindest, most caring man she'd ever met.

At his place tonight, she'd come perilously close to asking him to delay his trip to Boston, just for a few weeks—with no strings or commitments—to see if there was a chance for their relationship to become something more than it was now. Then her failure with Jeremy had flooded in, and she'd lost her nerve. She'd rather keep Ben as a friend forever than risk losing him altogether.

Although she'd managed to hold her ground against her growing feelings for him, it was the hardest thing she'd ever done. He'd generously taken the time to show her a different path than the one she'd chosen to follow, and she'd always be grateful to him. In her experience, people like Ben were the rarest kind of treasure.

Smiling at the screen, she prayed she'd get a chance to tell him so.

Was that a light?

In the oppressive darkness, Ben thought he'd seen a brief flash of light up ahead. The caves he'd searched so far were either empty or full of water, and he headed toward the faint bright spot he'd noticed. As he got closer, he noticed the outline of the cave and quickened his pace. It was nearly flooded, so he couldn't get in, but he climbed the outside and got a firm hold before angling around the front with his lantern.

"Ben?"

The sound of Lauren's voice, frightened but alive, washed over him like a sunbeam on a rainy day. Closing his eyes, he whispered a quick prayer of thanks. "Yeah, it's me. Are you okay?"

"More or less. There's an awful lot of water in here."

"I know. Hang on a minute. I'm gonna see if there's another way in." He ducked back, but returned when he heard her call out to him. "What?"

"Thank you for coming to find me. I was so scared…" Her voice wavered, then trailed off, telling him just how terrified she'd been. Out in the storm, all alone, thinking no one would ever find her. He couldn't begin to imagine it.

Hoping to bolster her spirits, he said, "Well, y'know, if I let anything happen to her Playtime director, your boss'd never let me hear the end of it."

That got him a shaky laugh, and he resumed hunting for another entrance to the cave. After a few minutes, he returned. "Do you want the good news first or the bad news?"

"Bad."

"There's no other way in."

She groaned. "Wonderful. What's the good news?"

"The storm's pulling out, and the tide's going with it. I'm guessing in a half hour or so you can walk right outta there."

"Okay."

She didn't sound thrilled about waiting, and he couldn't blame her. "I brought you a jacket, but I don't think it'll make it to you on its own. Gimme a sec."

He scrabbled around and found a decent-sized rock that weighed about five pounds. Taking off his top coat, he then removed the inner one, which was warm and dry. This he tied around the rock and lobbed it in to her. It hit the landing with a satisfying thud, telling him he'd hit the mark.

"Nice shot," she applauded, removing the coat she was wearing and pulling on the new one. Once she'd closed all the buckles and pulled up the hood, she sat back with a sigh. "Oh, that's fabulous. Thank you."

"Anytime."

"I'll be fine now. You don't have to wait here."

"Are you kidding me?" he scoffed. "I've been all over this beach trying to find you. I'm not going anywhere."

Brightening the cave with a grateful smile, she visibly relaxed. "Thank you. Again."

When he noticed her rubbing her ankle, he frowned. "You didn't say you were hurt."

"Oh, it's nothing. It was dark and the rocks were slippery, so I twisted my ankle. No big deal."

"We'll see about that."

"Don't—"

Before she could protest any further, Ben lifted the lantern over his head and plunged into chilly water that quickly sucked him in up to his chest. His father insisted he was part polar bear, which came in handy right now. Ignoring the cold, Ben half swam and half plowed through the small whirlpool until he got to the crude steps Lauren had obviously climbed to get to her rocky perch.

"Whew!" he exclaimed as he plunked himself down beside her. "That's cold even for me."

"You're insane, you know that?" Despite her scolding, she was beaming at him like he was some kind of hero. That adoring look did something funky to his insides, and he focused on her injured ankle to keep her from seeing his reaction.

"Well, it's not broken."

"That's good," she ground between clenched teeth. That told him it hurt more than she'd ever admit, which made him want to do something to ease her pain.

Rummaging around in the deep pockets of his jacket, he found a bandanna and used it to bind her swollen ankle. "I managed to get a call in to Mavis while I was up top. She said to tell you she's glad you're safe 'cause next time she sees you, she's gonna wring your pretty little neck."

He mimicked the keeper's gravelly voice, which made Lauren laugh. "I deserve that, I suppose."

Out in the harbor, the steady rhythm of the cutter's searchlight shifted into a series of co-ordinated blinks, and Lauren asked, "What's going on?"

"Everyone's out looking for you. They're

signaling with the light, to let 'em know you're safe and they can go home."

"You called out a search party for me?" When he nodded, she shook her head with a frown. "It never occurred to me my stupidity could bring other people out into this storm. I feel awful."

"A nice donation to the Holiday Harbor Search and Rescue Fund oughta square things."

"First thing in the morning," she promised. After a few moments of silence, she went on. "Can I tell you something that sounds totally nuts?"

It was good to hear the spunk coming back into her voice, and he grinned. "Sure."

"Before I thought I might actually die out here, it was amazing. All that power, completely wild and uncontrollable, knowing that the ocean's been doing this since the beginning of time and will go on doing it forever. It was—"

"Humbling," Ben filled in when she paused. "I know what you mean."

"You know what else is humbling? When I had no idea which cave would be safe, I asked God to help me find the right one." Fixing Ben with an earnest look, she added, "And He heard me. I'm not sure I'd have had the guts to wade into this dark hole in the wall if He hadn't given me a shove."

"And if you hadn't been in here, I probably wouldn't have noticed the light from your camera screen and would've kept hunting in the wrong place."

"After tonight, I'm convinced. I finally understand what it means to have faith, even when it's not easy." Resting her head back against the cave wall, she added, "I get it now."

He wondered if her new perspective included him, but decided this wasn't the right time to ask—if there ever was a right time—because she'd been through a lot tonight, he figured it was best to keep things light. "Better late than never."

She laughed again, and her voice sounded stronger when she said, "I have to tell you, in that getup you remind me of the guy on the fish-sticks box."

"Back at ya."

"But I'm much cuter."

He took the ribbing as a good sign. If Lauren felt confident enough to mess with him, she was fine. As for himself, the jury was still out. The thought of her being in so much danger had scared him more than anything in his life. Part of him believed that was a natural response to a sketchy situation, but the rest of him knew it for what it was.

Despite his best efforts, Lauren Foster had sneaked around his defenses and burrowed her way into his well-guarded heart. The question was, what was he going to do about it?

Chapter Ten

"Come on, Ben," Lauren chided impatiently from outside the velvet curtain. "Let me see it."

He'd been in there most of the morning, banging and tweaking, and a few times she'd heard the whine of his pneumatic screwdriver. The fact that she recognized the sound—and could name its source—was a clear sign she'd been spending way too much time with the man she only half-jokingly referred to as her hero. But she simply couldn't help it. The clock was ticking on his Boston plans, and in a couple of weeks he'd be gone. The old Lauren would have pulled away to avoid being hurt when he left.

The new Lauren wanted to tuck every precious moment with him away in her memory for safekeeping.

Finally, he stuck his head through the opening in the drapes, holding them close to his face to keep her from getting a glimpse of his finished project. "Ready?"

Lauren glared at her watch, then at him. "For an hour now. You're driving me nuts."

He chuckled, which was far from the reaction she'd been after. "City folks. Always in such a hurry."

"Listen, beach boy—"

"Beach boy," he echoed with a broad grin. "I like that. Makes me sound like a surfer or something."

Planting her hands on her hips, she actually growled at him, and he wisely took the hint. Tugging the pulleys he'd rigged up, he opened the curtains with the flourish of an enthusiastic summer-stock theater director.

Lauren was speechless. Even though she'd helped with some of the design and basic construction, the end product was exponentially more than she'd anticipated. The double-sided wardrobe looked like something straight out of a fairy tale, with a huge mirror bracketed on both sides with heavy tapestries. Pulling one aside, she found rows of various-sized cubby holes and baroque-style brass hooks, just waiting for all the costumes and accessories a princess could wish for.

Stepping up on the secure stage, the echo under her heels was the only clue that there was a huge sandbox underneath. The latches that secured it were burnished gold, making them look old and valuable when they were actually the latest in sturdy hardware.

When she reached out and released the catch on the huge carved wall, it pivoted almost effortlessly on the clever mechanism Ben had designed for it. On the other side were the angled shelves he'd promised, in all different sizes, ready for the fleet of trucks, excavators and bulldozers she'd ordered to fill them.

After taking it all in, she swiveled to look down at him. The look on his face was priceless, half excitement and half dread. How could he think for even a split second she wouldn't approve of what he'd done? It told her there was a current of vulnerability under that cocky exterior, and her heart softened just a little more toward him.

That was the ultimate in foolishness, and she quickly squashed it before it made her say something she couldn't take back. "It's perfect. Even better than I imagined."

Visibly relaxing, he let out a quick laugh. "Whew! I have to tell you, I wasn't sure how you'd like it. I mean, I thought it was cool, but—"

"It's the coolest," she assured him firmly. "Really, Ben. You've outdone yourself with this one, and the kids are all going to love it. I just wish you were going to be here while I'm setting up Jumping Beans."

She hadn't meant to say that out loud, and from his suddenly somber expression, it had taken him completely by surprise. "So you're going ahead with that?"

"I talked to Cooper yesterday, and he agreed to handle the closing for me. In return for a year's worth of drop-in child care," she added with a wink.

"Don't bother," Ben advised with a grin. "Everyone in town knows already."

"How? He said they just found out a few days ago."

"They made the mistake of telling Amelia. She's a sweetheart, but a vault of secrets—not so much."

They were both laughing when the bells over the door announced a customer. Still chuckling, Lauren called out, "Be right with you!"

She left Ben to his tweaking to greet whoever had come in for toys this morning. When she rounded the tall shelves she'd cowered behind not long ago, she stopped abruptly in midstep.

Their visitor turned to face her with the same disarming smile he'd been wearing the first time she met him. The smile that had come dangerously close to conning her into giving up her rights to her own life forever. "Hello, Lauren. It's good to see you."

Her brain had seized up like a rusty engine, but she quickly got a grip and kick-started it. "Jeremy."

She knew he was waiting for her to echo his "good to see you," but it would be a cold day on Maui when that happened. His disappointed frown confirmed her suspicion, and she congratulated herself on being slightly less predictable than he remembered. She'd made it through a wild Atlantic storm in one piece, she reminded herself. She could get through this, too.

That thought made her stand a little taller, and she came forward to where he stood, to prove she was no longer afraid of him. "What can I do for you?"

He smirked. "Don't you want to know how I found this jerkwater town you're in?"

"Not really."

"My paralegal is a celebrity nut," he continued as if she hadn't spoken. "She saw you in an online photo of Julia Stanton's wedding and showed it to me. After that, I did some research to find out where she was, and that led me to you."

A snarl was working its way up from the back of her throat, and she swallowed it down so her voice would come out normally. "How clever of you."

"Not clever, desperate." His customary arrogance gave way to a begging look. "Come home with me. I miss you."

Not long ago, his dramatic plea would have gotten to her. But these days, she saw him for what he was: a spoiled rich boy accustomed to having his own way. She wasn't a person to him, but a possession. During the long hours she'd spent with Ben and the other firmly grounded residents of Holiday Harbor, she'd learned the difference.

"This is my home now," she returned simply. "Have a good trip back to New York."

When she turned, he reached out to grab her arm. She'd expected the motion, but not her reflexive reaction to it. The old Lauren would have backpedalled to get out of his way. The new one glowered furiously and held her ground, jerking her arm free of his grasp. He was on her turf now, and she'd never back down to him—or anyone else—ever again.

"Get out, Jeremy. I'm not yours to yank around anymore."

"I never—"

"I'm pretty sure the lady just asked you to leave."

Lauren glanced back to find Ben leaning casually against a shelving unit full of military action figures. Arms folded, he made quite the picture standing there, apparently relaxed, but with those hard-work muscles ready to do whatever it took to send their unwelcome guest on his way. She must have been working in the toy store too long, because her main impression was that he fit right in with the commando units behind him.

Unfortunately, Jeremy was a lawyer accustomed to dealing with corporate crooks, and he wasn't about to be put off by the seemingly easygoing contractor. Offering a hand wrapped in a flashy gold bracelet, he gave his shark's smile. "I didn't realize anyone else was here. Jeremy Rutledge."

Ben didn't move an inch. Still, Lauren thought he looked bigger and more intimidating than he had a moment ago. After puzzling over the shift in his appearance, she realized it was his eyes. No longer the warm blue they'd been earlier, they were a threatening mix of blue and gray that brought to mind the storm that had thrashed its way up the coast the other night.

Any feelings she'd had for Jeremy had died long ago, but she still had no desire to watch Ben take him apart, either figuratively or literally. Hoping to dispel the palpable tension in the shop, she went to the door and opened it. "Goodbye, Jeremy."

He hesitated, glancing from her back to Ben, who still hadn't moved. "Is this the new guy?"

"Got a problem with that?" Ben demanded in a growl.

"Actually, yes. It seems her taste in men has gone alarmingly downhill."

"That's enough, Jeremy," she ordered to make it clear she was scolding him and not her knight in shining armor. All she wanted was for him to leave, but she had no idea how to make that happen. Then inspiration struck, and she said, "I'm curious about something. Back in New York, did you ever meet up with a lawyer named Cooper Landry?"

She was fairly confident there weren't a dozen attorneys with that name in the Big Apple, and judging by the color draining from Jeremy's face, he was well acquainted with the tenacious New Englander. "I did. Why?"

Never give anything away, Lauren mused with a slight grin. That was his style, but he didn't realize she'd learned a lot about him and now that she was no longer afraid of him, she could read him as easily as a children's story. "He's the mayor here now, and his office happens to be on the other side of that wall. What do you think he'd do if I called him over here to tell him about how you tried to take over my life?"

"I did no such thing," he insisted. "I gave you everything you asked for."

"You gave me everything you thought I should have," she corrected him calmly. "And when I didn't want it, you tried to bully me into taking it. All I needed was for you to love me, but now I understand you didn't know how."

His mouth fell open, but no sound came out. He looked like a landed fish gasping for air, and she pressed her lips into a firm line to suppress a triumphant smile. Finally, she'd outmanipulated the puppeteer who'd controlled her for far too long. It felt wonderful.

Finally, some of the color came back into his face, and he stammered, "I had no idea you were so unhappy."

"I'm not anymore. Have a good trip."

With that, she visually dismissed him and strolled over to the counter. She checked the computer screen and began typing as if she was responding to an email. In truth, nothing had come in, but her strategy had the desired effect. After remaining by the door for a few awkward moments, Jeremy turned and left the shop without another peep.

Once his luxury sedan had pulled away, Ben let out a low, appreciative whistle. "Very nice. Not many women can cut a guy off at the knees like that."

"Keep that in mind," she commented airily, sending him a mock warning glare.

"Yes, ma'am." He ambled over to the counter, pausing on the side opposite her. "Would you really do that? Call Cooper, I mean."

Lauren mulled that over for a second, then nodded. "Actually, I'm gonna do better than that. I'll have him file a restraining order against Jeremy. That way, if he ever gets the bright idea to come up here again, he'll think twice about it."

"Don't you both have to go in front of a judge for something like that?"

"Probably, but even starting the paperwork will send the message that I'm serious about keeping him away from me. If he tests me, he won't like the result. And neither will the partners at his firm," she added with more than a little venom.

A slow, admiring smile brightened Ben's face. "Good for you."

Very good for her, she thought proudly. Holiday Harbor was her home, and she wasn't going to live in fear of Jeremy showing up out of the blue like that in the future. She'd overcome her old reticence and defeated him on her own. The knowledge that she could do it again made her feel stronger than she ever had.

"Thanks for the backup, by the way. Most people assume I'm a fragile girl who needs to be taken care of, so I really appreciate you letting me fight my own battle."

The grin widened, and mischief twinkled in his eyes. "No problem, Rapunzel."

She knew he was ribbing her, so she laughed. "Of course, it went better with a big, nasty guy lurking in the background."

"Nasty? Is that how I looked?"

"Actually, you looked like you wanted to rip him apart with your bare hands," she informed him with a grateful smile. "If I didn't know you as well as I do, I'd have been pretty terrified."

"But you do know me." Reaching across the counter, he gently took her hands in his strong, capable ones. His bemused expression had given way to a warm gaze, and he added, "I'd never do anything to hurt you, Lauren. You have my word on that."

His promise was made with a blend of

affection and something else Lauren needed a few moments to identify: respect. That was when she recognized that while other people here viewed her the same way, no one in New York ever had. Or in Philly, she reluctantly admitted. Oh, some of them might like her well enough, but even her own parents had never seen her as a mature, capable person. She was a pretty girl with a bright personality and a murky future. Nothing more, nothing less.

What was different now? she wondered. Even before the question finished forming in her mind, she knew the answer. It was faith. Now that she'd reconnected with God, she'd tapped into a vein of strength she'd always had inside her but had never utilized. Beyond that, she knew He'd given her a brain so she could use it to make her life what He'd meant for it to be.

Gazing at the man who'd taught her what it meant to truly care for someone, she smiled. "I know that, Ben, and it means a lot to me."

You mean a lot to me, she nearly blurted before stopping herself.

"I'm real glad to hear that. I'd say shedding Jeremy for good calls for a celebration."

"Like what?"

Pulling his hands away, he crossed his arms on the counter with a mischievous grin. "Well, since I'm your boyfriend now," his eyes twinkled merrily at the joke, "I've got a few ideas."

"I'm sure." Unable to resist this irresistible man any longer, she rested her arms on the other side of the divider and leaned toward him. "Like what?"

"Dinner at The Crow's Nest. My treat."

"Are you finally asking me out on a real date, after all this time?"

"Seeing as you just gave your ex the official boot, I figured it's okay." Cocking his head in that pose she'd come to adore, he fixed her with a warm, promising smile. "Whattya say?"

"Does any woman over twenty and breathing ever say no to you?"

Squinting up at the ceiling, he made a show of considering her question very seriously. But when he met her gaze, his eyes crinkled with humor. "Nope."

Letting out a melodramatic sigh, Lauren went along. "Well, I'd hate to be the one to break your streak."

"Thanks. I appreciate that."

With a quick kiss on her cheek, he sauntered out the door whistling an upbeat song she vaguely recognized as a Beach Boys tune. Probably because she'd called him that earlier, she decided with a smile. As she watched him go, she shook her head with a sigh.

"Great going, Lauren," she chided herself out loud. "Now you've really done it."

"I don't see what the big deal is," Eric muttered while Ben finished getting ready for his date with Lauren. "It's just dinner."

"It's a big deal because when I met her, she wouldn't get within five feet of me," Ben explained patiently. Now that he'd gotten a firsthand view of Jeremy Rutledge, he was convinced that Lauren's fear of him had been completely justified. The slimy attorney was the worst example of male heavy-handedness, and recalling their tense encounter made Ben angry all over again. "She trusts me, and I don't want to mess that up."

Eric remained quiet for a minute, then he made an "aha" kind of noise and chuckled. "You're in love with her."

"What? Of course not." Even to his own ears, Ben's protest sounded almost violent, and he dialed it back a notch. "But she's kinda fragile, and I don't want to do anything to send her back into her shell again."

"You mean like rescuing her from drowning in one of those old sea caves? Your biggest worry's probably how to keep her from figuring out you're more Clark Kent than Superman."

Making a face, Ben whipped one of his mismatched socks at his sarcastic houseguest. "Thanks a lot."

"You gotta watch that hero stuff, little brother," Eric cautioned as he strode from the room. "It's gonna get you in trouble one of these days."

Unfortunately, that day seemed to be today, Ben mused while he settled the collar of his striped button-down and assessed his reflection. In spite of his wholehearted intention to keep his distance from Julia's gorgeous but perplexing visitor, he'd managed to bungle his way closer and closer.

And now, with the deadline for starting on Davy's crew rapidly approaching, Ben was seriously torn about taking the job. If he stayed in Holiday Harbor, he could work on the Jumping Beans rehab with Lauren and make the name Thomas and Sons a reality again. After tonight, he'd have a better idea if things between Lauren and him could really go anywhere, or if this was all just his imagination.

In all honesty, he wasn't sure which option suited him better. His instincts told him a lasting relationship with Lauren would be amazing but complicated. Restoring old build-

ings—his dream for as long as he could remember—would be rewarding and much
easier to manage.

As he trotted downstairs and out to his
truck, he couldn't help wondering why Eric
had immediately gone to the "in love" as-
sessment. For weeks now, folks all over town
who'd known him his entire life had clumsily
attempted to entangle him with their lovely
visitor. Did they see something between the
two of them that he didn't? Or was it just
wishful thinking on their part because they
assumed he was lonely? Since he didn't have
an answer for either question, he put them
aside and made the short drive to Toyland.

Lauren was waiting for him, sitting in the
shade of a leafy oak on one of the park benches
out front of Toyland. When he parked and got
out, her face swung toward him, and the incredible smile she gave him nearly knocked
the breath out of him.

With each step he took toward her, Boston
faded a little more into the background, taking his professional dreams right along with
it. Lauren might end up being everything he'd
ever need, but to find out, he'd have to give
up the one thing he'd always wanted. And if
things went sour between them, he and his
broken heart would be right back where they

started, stuck in a dead-end job in a small town whose biggest claim to fame was that it was too stubborn to be washed out to sea.

Dressed to the nines in a slim black cocktail dress and heels, she looked better suited to Manhattan than Maine, and he marveled at the changes in her since she arrived. They had nothing to do with makeup or clothes, and he quickly pegged the major difference: confidence. Now she had all of it she needed, and it made her even more beautiful than ever.

When it occurred to him he was standing on the sidewalk basically gawking at her, he called up a crooked grin. "Sorry to be staring. You look fantastic."

That got him the sparkling laugh she used so rarely. "Thank you. I was hoping it wasn't because I had on two different earrings."

"You're wearing earrings?" he teased, happy to hear that laugh again. "It's a good thing I've got a six-foot level behind the driver's seat. When the guys at the restaurant get a look at you, I'm gonna need something to fight 'em off with."

"I think you already did that today," she reminded him with a grateful smile.

"No, that was all you. I was just backing you up. Not that you needed it."

She chewed on that for a few seconds, then

nodded. "You're right, I didn't. It felt good to put him in his place that way. I should've done it a long time ago."

Ben was about to say something when he noticed her staring openmouthed at something going on at the other end of the street.

"Are those guys wheeling in old bathtubs?" When he glanced over and nodded, she continued, "What are they doing on Main Street?"

"They have to measure 'em, so they know how many will fit widthwise."

Clearly still baffled, she asked the obvious question. "Why?"

"Memorial Day is the first holiday of the summer, and every year we have a big town celebration. It starts with the Costume Regatta out on the bay."

"Don't tell me," she interrupted with a knowing grin. "People dress up their boats for the race."

"You got it. Anyway, after that we come up here for the parade and some kind of race. We've had rowboats, shopping carts, even baby strollers. This year it's those," he finished, motioning toward the ancient cast-iron tubs several men were shoving onto wheeled dollies.

"And you're running."

"Well, me and some friends. Bree's the

lightest member of the team, so she's sitting in the tub while Cooper, Nick and I push."

"Your mayor's going to race a bathtub down Main Street on Memorial Day," she summed it up with a grin. "I must be getting used to this place, because that doesn't shock me even the tiniest bit."

"Then you won't be surprised when we take the trophy."

"You sound pretty sure of yourself. What makes you so confident you're going to win?"

Glancing around to make sure no one was eavesdropping, he leaned in and whispered, "We've got a secret weapon. We're a lock."

Clearly intrigued, she pressed closer and murmured, "What is it?"

"Sorry, no previews. But last week I thought of something nobody's ever tried before, and it's gonna win us that race."

"I'll take your word for it, then." She was quiet for a few moments, and then she laughed. "I'm trying to picture the mayor of Philadelphia doing something like this, but I can't."

"Well, Cooper's not your average public official," Ben reminded her. When the man in question spotted them on the sidewalk, he waved and hurried over. "Uh-oh. This can't be good."

"What makes you say that?"

"He never hurries for anything."

When Cooper joined them, he greeted them with, "Man, am I glad to see you two. We've got a problem for the race."

Ben frowned. "What's wrong?"

"Nothing terrible, but Bree's morning sickness has expanded into morning-noon-and-night sickness. She can hardly stand up right now, so there's no way she can be our fourth next Monday."

"That's horrible," Lauren said with obvious concern. "Can she eat anything at all?"

"Sure, she just can't keep it down." Catching himself, Cooper frowned. "Sorry. That's probably more than you wanted to know."

"I'm sorry she's feeling so awful," Lauren continued. "Is she up for some distracting company?"

"Not just yet, but I'll tell her you asked. She'll appreciate it. Right now, it's best to tiptoe around and leave her be," he added in the voice of a man who'd learned that from unpleasant personal experience.

While he shared Lauren's sympathy for the sick Mrs. Landry, Ben's mind had been working on the race issue. A solution popped into his head, and he glanced over at Lauren. "You look like you're pretty light."

"Thanks." Evidently, she figured out the

meaning behind his compliment, because she laughed. "You want me to ride in your stinky old bathtub, don't you?"

"It's not stinky," he protested. "I pulled it from my house and cleaned it out real well. It's good as new, trust me."

Something unusual sparkled in her eyes, and she said, "I do."

Somehow, those words sounded just right coming from her. It was a sweet, intimate kind of moment, and in Ben's opinion, it passed by much too fast.

Keenly aware that Cooper was eyeing them with more curiosity than normal, Ben forced a chuckle. "Great, then it's a go. Thanks for helping us out."

Looking back to Cooper, she asked, "What do I get when we win?"

"Tell you what," he replied with a laugh. "We'll split the trophy between your shop and my reception area, six months each."

"Deal." After they shook on it, she turned to Ben. "Ready for dinner?"

"Always."

He held out a hand for her, and for the first time, she took it. As if that wasn't enough, she held his arm and leaned against him in a show of faith that actually made his chest ache.

Oh, yeah, he thought as they made their way down the walkway to The Crow's Nest. He was a goner.

Chapter Eleven

"So," Lauren nudged while they dug into their scrumptious lobster salad, "now that I'm on the team, can you tell me about our secret weapon?"

Again, he did the spy-checking thing. Then he leaned closer and very seriously said, "Nope."

"Oh, come on! You can trust me."

"I know that, but we want it to be a shocker for everyone. It's epic, and we don't want to ruin the effect by letting the cat out of the bag ahead of time."

"Does Bree know?"

Grinning, he shook his head. "And neither does Julia. Us guys made a pact—spit-shook and everything."

Lauren wrinkled her nose in distaste. "Eww. Boys are so disgusting."

"Yeah, well, we come in handy when you need something heavy carried in, don't we?"

"I guess. Speaking of handy," she added, slipping her new purchase from her purse. "Look what I bought at the wireless store in Oakbridge this afternoon."

"Cute," he approved in between bites. "I especially like the jazzy pink case. Very girlie."

"I had the guy turn off the tracking feature first thing, just to be on the safe side. Jeremy's a sly one, and I don't want him trying that trick again."

After swallowing, Ben scowled. "I don't normally say things like this, but I really hate that guy. He should be glad I didn't toss him right through that bay window onto the street."

She gasped. "With all that glass? Do you know what a mess that would make?"

He shrugged as if that detail didn't concern him in the least. "I'm a contractor. When things are broken, I fix 'em."

Not just things, Lauren added silently, *but people, too.* He'd stood by his father and brother through some tough times, and now both of them were doing well. Then there was her.

When she arrived in Holiday Harbor, she was a terrified, shattered woman who had no idea what tomorrow would bring. Then Ben strode into her life, and with patient understanding, he'd helped her gather up the pieces of herself and reassemble them into someone much stronger. Someone who could take the curves life threw her way and make them work.

There weren't words to thank him properly for all he'd done, so she settled for her biggest, brightest smile. "Yes, you do. And very well, too."

That got her a puzzled look, then understanding dawned in his expressive eyes. "You're not just talking about windows, are you?"

Reaching across the table, she rested her hand over his. It was the first time she'd initiated contact between them, and a little thrill zipped up her spine. Whether it was the sensation of touching him or the boldness it had taken to do it, she wasn't sure, but it felt incredible. "I couldn't ask for better than you've given me, Ben. If it weren't for you, I'd still be slinking around with my head down, hoping no one would notice me."

"I doubt that," he returned with an approving grin, "but thanks for saying it, anyway." Their waitress returned, and after she left their tureen of steaming seafood bisque, he went on.

"So tell me about Jumping Beans. How're the arrangements coming along?"

"Slow, but fine. My small-business loan came through, and Cooper's handling the real estate and incorporation stuff. I registered for the next round of certification classes, so that part will be done soon. Oh, and yesterday I came up with a great idea for designing the logo." Reaching into her bag again, she pulled a postcard from the stack she'd picked up from the printer earlier. Handing it to him, she explained, "I'm gonna let the kids who shop at Toyland do drawings and enter them in a contest. The one I pick will get a free Playtime party for them and five of their friends."

"Awesome idea," he approved, handing the card back.

"I thought so." Lifting the cover from the bisque, she ladled out some for each of them. "What about Boston? Your job starts in a few days, but you haven't said much about it lately."

He shrugged. "Not much to tell. Old house, big crew, lots of work."

His lack of enthusiasm baffled her, and she pressed. "It sounds like you're not as eager to go as you were a few weeks ago."

Another shrug, but she noticed he refused to meet her eyes. That wasn't like him, and she wondered if he was having second thoughts about going so far from his hometown. "Is there a project around here you could work on instead?"

"Not that I know of. Besides, I really want to see some of the world, y'know? Dad never got the chance to do that, and he regrets it."

It sounded like he was trying to convince himself as much as her, but that made no sense at all. Following the twists in this conversation was making her dizzy. "But he's happy now, right?"

"Sure, but it took him a while to get there." Sighing, Ben added, "It's just that there aren't many historical rehab options around here, and in other places there are plenty."

"So basically, it's time to either go after your dream or give up on it."

"Yeah."

Judging by his downcast attitude, he wasn't any crazier about leaving than she was to have him go. She'd come to rely on him, on his calm, steady presence and his sunny disposition that could brighten even the darkest day. He'd guided her through the worst time of her life, and when she finally came out the other side, he'd cheerfully given her a shove and let her go. She couldn't envision any of the other men she'd known having the generosity and strength to do that, and that was when she knew....

She was in love with him.

The revelation hit her with the force of a coastal hurricane, and she actually sat back in her chair to regain her composure. Ben must have noticed, because he sent her a worried look. "You okay?"

She didn't trust herself to speak normally, so she nodded until her pulse settled a bit. "This broth is really something."

"Lemons," he explained with a chuckle. "I don't know where they're from, but they sure do pack a wallop."

Forcing a smile, she sipped some water to cover her suddenly unpredictable emotions. Fortunately, he kept up the conversation while she recovered.

"I've been thinking," he said while he swirled his spoon through the pool of butter sauce on his plate. Meeting her gaze, he looked more serious than she'd ever seen him. "Maybe there's a third option for me."

"Really?" she almost squeaked, clearing her throat so she wouldn't sound like a twit. "What's that?"

"A different dream," he replied quietly, never taking his eyes from hers. "A better one."

Did he mean her? Lauren wondered as her

heart leaped into her throat. Could this wonderful man possibly be considering giving up the job he wanted more than anything to stay in Holiday Harbor with her?

Exciting as that prospect was, she feared that if he stayed for her, eventually he'd resent it and they'd be miserable. Or things between them would go sour and she'd be crushed. Either way, it was a lose-lose situation for her, and while she was much more self-assured than she used to be, she simply didn't have what it took to take a leap like that.

So, in the interest of her sanity, she put aside her foolish wishes and deftly changed the subject.

After Ben dropped Lauren off at her place, he was too restless to go straight home. He'd hoped the dinner out with her would satisfy his curiosity about how it would be to seriously date her. Unfortunately for him, it had done the opposite. It had taken all his considerable willpower not to ask her out again. Even though he was leaving next week, part of him longed to wring the most out of every moment he could spend with her.

Another part was seriously considering calling Davy and telling him he'd changed his mind about Boston. After all these years of praying and waiting for a chance to leave his hometown, Ben couldn't believe he was even thinking of staying. And for what? A woman?

Not just any woman, he amended with a little grin. An amazing one who challenged him at every turn and fascinated him beyond reason. More than beautiful, Lauren had brains and drive, and a healthy sense of what she wanted out of life. Ben was confident he could be the man she chose to share that life with. He just had to put aside his old dream and embrace a new one with her.

Recognizing he needed advice on this one, Ben did something that only a month ago he'd have regarded as an idiotic waste of time. He drove to his father's house to ask for his help. The lights were on, and Dad's pickup was the only car in the driveway, so Ben pulled in behind it.

A knock on the door brought him in from the living room, and Ben waved through the screen. "Have you got a minute?"

"Always. Come on in."

The place was neat as a pin and smelled like lemon-scented furniture polish. Even the windows were spotless, and Ben eyed his father with a knowing smile. "Amelia's been here, I see."

"It's not what you're thinking. I traded her

some housecleaning for building a new potting shed for her garden."

"Actually, Dad, I was thinking something exactly like that. Mind if I sit down?"

"Of course not." He motioned to the kitchen table. "I've got some leftover beef stew. Are you hungry?"

"No, thanks. I just stuffed myself to the gills at The Crow's Nest. With Lauren," he added to get the ball rolling.

It was Dad's turn for the knowing smile. "And how's that going?"

"Too well." Groaning, Ben stared up at the ceiling as if that would help. "I don't know what came over me, asking her out this way. It's just making things harder."

"What things? If you enjoy spending time together, that's good."

He could tell from Dad's puzzled tone that he wasn't making any sense. That figured, since he didn't get it, either. With a heavy sigh, he met his father's worried eyes. "I'm not sure I wanna go to Boston."

A smile flickered at the corner of his dad's mouth, and he nodded in understanding. "And that's what's making things harder. You have to choose between the job you want and the woman you want."

"She's not like anyone I've ever known." Hearing the desperation in his voice, Ben cringed but kept going. "She's beautiful and smart, and she messes with me constantly. I don't know why, but I like it."

"And you'd miss it if you were so far away." When Ben nodded, Dad leaned back in his chair and crossed his arms. "Let me ask you this. If you stay here, what's the downside?"

"There's no historical project going on."

"And what's the upside?"

Ben's smile pushed up from somewhere deep inside him, and even though he knew he must look like a lovesick teenager, he didn't even try to stop it. "Lauren."

"I'd say that's your answer, son. Your heart's telling you to stay here in Holiday Harbor and give things with Lauren a chance."

"What if they go bad?"

"Like with me and your mom, you mean?" Ben started to protest, but Dad stopped him with a hand in the air. "I can handle it now. Amelia helped me see that your mother was never meant to be here forever, and I have to accept that. I'll always love her, but it's time for me to get on with my life. It's tough, but if you had to, you'd get through it, too. Boston's full of historic buildings that have been around for over two hundred years. They're not going anywhere."

"So you're saying I should stay here and take a shot with Lauren?"

"I think you should listen to your heart," he clarified with a sage look. "It knows what's best for you, even when your brain gets in the way."

Spoken with the wisdom of hard-won experience, his father's words struck a chord in Ben, and he nodded. "The only question is, does she want the same thing?"

"Only she can answer that. And that means you have to ask."

Ben had never done anything even remotely like what his father was suggesting, and the prospect of it didn't exactly fill him with confidence. Pushing off from the table, he said, "Thanks for the advice, Dad. I'll think about it."

"Give your heart a chance, too," he cautioned as they walked to the door. "Jobs can wait, but sometimes people can't."

No truer words had ever been spoken in their house, Ben mused while he got into his truck and headed for home. The problem was, he wasn't sure he was ready to make that move just yet. Rushing would ruin his opportunity for a lasting relationship with Lauren, but waiting too long would have the same result.

No closer to a decision than he'd been half an hour ago, Ben drove home in the worst funk of his life.

* * *

Memorial Day was a big deal in Holiday Harbor.

The whole town was done up in red-white-and-blue bunting, with flags flying from any-place that had room for a pole. Lauren half expected the cast of *Yankee Doodle Dandy* to appear in the gazebo and begin singing their famous theme song.

The festivities started at eight o'clock, down at the harbor. With the famous Last Chance Lighthouse in the background, sailboats and rowboats of all sizes lined up near a set of buoys that marked the start and finish of the Costume Regatta. Ben hadn't been teasing, she quickly realized as she settled on a bench to watch.

The crews were dressed up in all kinds of costumes, from patriotic to downright odd. Most of their vessels were decked out, too, and a couple of them even had faces added to the front. The bow, she corrected herself while she sipped her coffee. If she was going to live in a fishing village, she had to get a handle on the lingo.

"Morning." Lauren glanced up to find Bree standing there, a little green but basically on her feet. "Do you mind if I sit with you?"

Lauren patted the bench with a smile. "Not a bit. How are you feeling?"

"One step up from bilge water," her new friend shot back with a wry grin. "But Cooper and Sammy are racing, and I wouldn't miss this for anything."

"Sammy?" Lauren echoed. "Is that a friend of his?"

"More or less. He's a huge black Newfie Cooper rescued last year, and when Cooper takes the boat out, that dog is right beside him. I think they're both happier out on the water than on dry land."

Her fond smile faded, and she suddenly went very pale. From her deep breath, Lauren assumed she was fighting off a wave of nausea. When it seemed to have passed, she asked, "Can I get you anything?"

"No, thanks. I've been living on saltines and ginger ale the last week, and even the thought of anything else makes me queasy. I have to leave before the food tents get cranked up, so don't be offended if I run off without saying goodbye."

"Gotcha." Out of sympathy for Bree, Lauren tossed her latte into a nearby trash can.

While waiting for the race to start they chatted pleasantly about goings-on around town, and the Martins stopped to say good morning.

"Happy Memorial Day, everyone," Lauren replied, adding a smile for Hannah. "There's my favorite marketing director."

Hannah's bright smile made Lauren's day. "I just did the picture. You're doing everything else."

"Before the party, I was hoping you'd help me get Jumping Beans set up so you and your friends will have fun there. It's been a long time since I was your age."

"Sure," she breathed, eyes wide, as her ponytail bobbed with excitement. "Wait till I tell Uncle Nick and Aunt Julia I'm gonna be a market rector."

A low chuckle sounded behind them, and Lauren glanced up to find the uncle and aunt in question standing on the sidewalk. "Marketing director, munchkin. If you're gonna do the job, you need to say it right."

Squealing with delight, she launched herself into Nick's arms, reaching over to hug Julia at the same time. "I missed you so-o-o much. Did you see any whales? Did you get to feed a polar bear? How many dogs were pulling the sled you rode on?"

Patiently, Julia said, "We saw lots of whales, but it's dangerous to feed polar bears. There were eight dogs on our team, and we even got to play with some of their puppies. We have pictures of everything, and we'll show them to you all later."

"Awesome! Me and Mommy kept an eye on Lauren while you were gone, just like you asked me to."

Laughing, Lauren said, "So that's why everything went so well. Thank you, Hannah."

"I'm sorry to break up the reunion," Lainie interrupted, holding out a hand for her bubbly daughter. "We have to get to the parade starting line. We'll catch up with all of you later."

"I'm marching with our 4-H group," Hannah informed everyone proudly. "Sammy's pulling our wagon, and I have to make sure he does it right."

Lauren chuckled. "How on earth did you convince a dog to do something like that?"

"He'll do anything for Hannah," Nick explained. "So he's pulling a wagon with ducks and chickens in it."

Anywhere else, Lauren would have thought that was unusual. In Holiday Harbor, though, it was just par for the course. "We'll catch up with you later, then. Have fun."

"You, too!" Hannah called, waving as she hurried away with Lainie rushing to catch up.

Nick groaned as he threw himself onto the bench beside Julia. "I love that girl, but I don't know how Lainie does it. She'd wear me out in a day."

"You get used to it," Todd told him while he angled Noah's stroller for a good view.

"Between the two of them, when do you sleep?"

"When they're older," his brother-in-law replied with a grin.

"Thanks for the warning," Nick grumbled just as she noticed the Thomases making their way down the ramp toward the water.

Lauren hadn't seen much of Ben since their dinner the other night, and she'd assumed he was busy preparing for his big move to Boston. He was leaving tomorrow, so he must have a lot to do. Still, she'd been wishing they could have some more time together before that happened. Apparently, he didn't share that wish.

There was no more room on the benches, so the family greeted everyone before heading farther down the dock. Except for Ben, who for some odd reason stayed behind even though there was no place for him to sit.

"I just love how the Playtime area turned out," Julia gushed. "You and Lauren did a wonderful job."

"Yeah, we make a good team." Flashing Lauren a quick smile, he sprawled out on the weathered planks in front of her like a loyal golden retriever. Tipping his head back, he said, "Morning, sunshine."

She loved the way that sounded, and her murky mood improved considerably. "Morning. How's your packing coming along?"

"Nice day for a race."

He'd neatly sidestepped her question, and she wasn't sure what to make of that. But since he clearly didn't want to discuss his upcoming trip, she figured it was best to go along. "And for riding in a bathtub."

That got her one of those slow, mischievous grins of his, and she couldn't help laughing. "You're still not gonna tell me your big secret, are you?"

"Nope."

She angled a look at Nick, who stared back at her with the most deadpan expression she'd ever seen. "And don't start whispering with my wife. She doesn't know, either."

"A bunch of macho nonsense, I'm sure," Julia huffed, but her adoring smile gave her away.

Seeing her old friend so happy no longer made Lauren envious, she realized with a start. It gave her hope for her own future, and who might be part of it. That thought led her to the man seated at her feet, and she fought the urge to grab those broad shoulders and hold on tight to keep him from leaving. She'd never wanted anything more than she wanted him to stay and see if they could build a life together in this charming town on the edge of the sea.

She'd never tell him that, of course. She didn't want him to miss out on the opportunity of a lifetime because of her. They had one more day together, she reminded herself sternly. She wasn't about to do anything to spoil it.

The race was a short one, mostly because it was the first event in a long day of celebrating. Cooper and Sammy came in a close second, which Bree assured them all was part of the plan. Capable of winning every one of the six races held each year, he threw two out of three to allow someone else the joy of hoisting the trophy once in a while.

Once all the boats were secured at the dock, sailors and spectators alike trooped up to find seats for the parade. Born and raised in Philadelphia, Lauren had grown up surrounded by America's proud history. Their parades were large and lavish, so she wasn't sure what to expect from this one. What she got was far beyond anything she could have imagined.

A Revolutionary War color guard started things off, dressed in period costumes and playing an upbeat military tune on antique instruments. The flag they carried looked like it had been around as long as the town, and when they stopped in the middle of Main Street, every hat came off. A man with a fabulous tenor voice stepped out from the ranks to sing "The Star-Spangled Banner," and Lauren joined in with everyone else along the route. It was a touching, patriotic moment that seemed ideal for this quaint place.

Behind them came the school's marching band and a group of people in old-fashioned costumes riding high-wheel bikes. Around the corner, Lauren caught sight of good-natured Sammy, his black fur brushed and shining while he calmly pulled a wagon full of caged birds. Hannah walked beside him, patting him and slipping him a treat every chance she got. It was absolutely adorable, and Lauren snapped several pictures before they disappeared from view.

When the horseback contingent appeared, Ben and Nick got to their feet.

"We should get going," Ben said, offering Lauren his hand. "The race'll start as soon as they clean up from the horses."

"Good planning," Lauren joked, hoping her nervousness wasn't too obvious. She still had no idea what their secret weapon was, and whether it would win them the race or land her on the pavement in a bruised heap.

"You be careful with my girl," Julia warned them sternly. "I like her in one piece."

"Yeah," Lauren agreed as they hurried away. "Me, too."

"On your marks…" the Bakery Sisters shouted in unison. "Get set… Go!"

Within a matter of seconds, ten bathtubs mounted on wheeled carts got underway. There were modern ones, claw-foot ones like Lauren was riding in, even a stand-up shower. The rules were simple: one person rides, three others push. The first team to go the length of Main Street and back to the start/finish line was the winner.

For some reason, Cooper, Nick and Ben seemed to be dogging behind her, and Lauren glanced over her shoulder to find them all grinning at each other. They had something up their sleeves, and she couldn't wait to find out what it was. At the turn, she finally got her answer.

While the other crews traveled far past the mark and laboriously wheeled their tubs around, the guys behind her simply jumped to the front of their tub and began pushing it back the way they'd come. Some in the crowd began cheering, others booing, and the noise echoing between the tall buildings was deafening.

They crossed the finish line far ahead of the runners-up, and almost immediately, the arguing started.

"That's not fair!" someone yelled.

"Pretty clever," another chimed in.

While people debated whether the win was legitimate or not, things got pretty heated. You'd have thought someone had sneaked away with a solid gold winner's cup, not a handmade trophy that circulated with each race. Before long, the other team captains had circled around her tub, so Lauren couldn't have gotten out if she wanted to. Which she didn't. Delighted to be in the middle of the action, she pulled her knees up and waited to see what would happen.

"Cooper, you're the mayor," one man pointed out. "You should know better than to pull a stunt like this."

"I thoroughly reviewed the rules," he responded in a calm, courtroom kind of voice. "Nowhere do they say that the tub has to be pushed from the same handholds up and back."

"I'd like to see that for myself, if you don't mind," another man insisted.

Cooper must have been a Boy Scout, because he smiled and took a folded sheet of paper from the back pocket of his jeans. While people huddled around to read the few lines it contained, Ben broke through the commotion and came over to lean his arms on the rolled side of the tub.

"So…" he began with a proud grin. "Whaddya think?"

"I think you're brilliant," she returned without hesitation. "Now get me outta this thing."

"Yes, ma'am."

Reaching up, he grasped her around the waist, holding her steady until her feet were back on solid ground. Then, without warning, he gathered her into his arms for a long, heady kiss. It stunned her so completely that when he finally let go, all she could do was stare up at him and blink.

"I need to talk to you," he murmured into her ear.

"Um…okay."

Taking her hand, he led her away from the ongoing discussion about whether the race could officially be called or not. Crossing the street, they skirted around the vendor tents and headed for the gazebo, which was currently the only unoccupied place in the square.

Ben motioned for her to sit, and she sank onto the bench, her mind racing to guess what he might be gearing up to say. All morning, she'd been getting the impression that he had something important to tell her but was waiting for the right moment. Apparently, this was it.

He paced a few steps each way, then turned and stared down at her. Those amazing blue eyes shone with something she couldn't identify, and hokey as it was, she thought her heart actually skipped a beat. When he finally sat beside her, she braced herself for some kind of bombshell.

"What would you say," he began in a careful tone, "if I told you I was thinking about *not* going to Boston?"

She squeaked then cleared her throat for a more coherent response. "I'd ask you why."

Looking down, he took her hand loosely in his then met her eyes again. "Because I think maybe I'm in love with you."

Gasping, she threw her arms around him in an impulsive hug, not caring that anyone with a working set of eyes could see them. When he gathered her closer, she marveled at how right it felt to be wrapped in his arms, treasured and protected from anything that might harm her. Resting her cheek on his shoulder, she sighed. "I'd say that's good, because I think maybe I'm in love with you, too."

Pulling away, he gently held her at arm's

length. "You're sure about this? I mean, we could end up hating each other in a month."

"Or we could end up loving each other forever," she suggested with a smile. "If we don't try, we'll never know."

Returning her smile, he kissed her again then rested his forehead against hers with a sigh. "Y'know, you kinda ruined the moment. I thought I'd have to convince you, and I had this whole speech all planned out."

"Is that why you haven't called me?"

"Yeah." His face a study in misery, he explained, "I wasn't sure you felt the same way I did, and it took me a while to figure out how to ask."

"Aw, poor baby." Laughing, she got up and tugged him to his feet. Slipping her arms around his waist, she suggested, "How 'bout if later you give me the rest of the spiel? I'll let you know if it would've worked."

"You mean like tomorrow?" A playful glint lit his eyes. "When I'm not driving to Boston?"

Beaming at the man who'd stood by her from the first moment she met him, she nodded. "Tomorrow."

Epilogue

"To Jumping Beans!" Ben shouted, lifting his grape-juice box in a toast.

"Thank you so much for coming, everyone," Lauren added. "It's been a long three months, but thanks to my awesome contractors—" she saluted the three Thomas men "—we're finally ready for kids. By the time school opens, I hope this place will really be hopping."

"You mean jumping, don't you?" Hannah asked, making everyone laugh.

"Yes, I do, and thanks for reminding me. I never could've made this place work without all that help from you and your friends."

"We had fun," the little girl assured her. "I can't wait to come here when kindergarten's over."

A fresh cookie tray appeared, and Hannah zoomed off to check out the new selection of treats. Lauren circulated among her guests, including friends and families she'd invited to check out Holiday Harbor's latest business. Some children would attend full-time, some part-time, and others would have fun before and after school while they waited for the school bus or for their parents to pick them up. Even though it was housed in a century-old former candy shop, Jumping Beans was a bright, airy place filled with mats, toys, puzzles and a top-notch art area outfitted with easels and smocks.

Lauren had designed it with Ben's pragmatic help, and together they'd overseen every aspect of its creation. Tonight, she was opening the doors for the first time, and people were flooding in to see the results. Judging by the rapidly filling interest sheet, she'd be at max capacity by the time school started. That meant it was time to start pruning her list of potential employees, but tomorrow was soon enough for that. Tonight, she was just going to enjoy herself.

When she had a free moment, she paused to get a cup of water from the cooler whose wooden stand was shaped like a stegosaurus. One of Ben's more creative ideas, it was her favorite piece in the building.

"Hey there, sunshine," he greeted her with a wide grin and a peck on the cheek. "Great party."

"I'm thrilled so many people showed up. You never know what you'll get with something like this. It can be a big hit or you might be stuck with trays full of tiny sandwiches."

"Can I talk to you a sec?"

Lifting her bangs, she ran the cup over her warm forehead. "Sure. What did you need?"

"Not here."

His eager expression alerted her that something was up. Over the summer, she'd learned he was fond of surprises. Even better, she'd learned she was fond of getting them, so she took the hand he offered her and followed him out the emergency door into the fenced side yard.

There, surrounded by bright plastic playground toys, he said, "I got some interesting news from Cooper today."

"Really? What's that?"

"There's a new historical restoration starting up over in Oakbridge. Seems they found out one of those creaky old houses belonged to some pirate-turned-naval-hero who outfoxed the British during the War of 1812. Cooper heard about it and did some research. Apparently, it's a legit landmark reclamation project, approved and funded by the state, and he recommended me for the crew."

"And you got the job, of course. I'm so proud of you!" Since that wasn't nearly enough, she embraced him for good measure. "This is the answer to your prayers. You can be here and still work on your dream job."

"It's pretty cool, but I'll also have to do a lot of studying to get myself up to speed before we start the interiors in October. The other guys have been doing this kinda thing for years, and I've got a lot of catching up to do so I don't mess anything up. I'm afraid that means I won't have a lot of spare time this fall," he added in a hesitant tone.

"Oh, I understand. I'll be crazy then, I'm sure, working out the kinks with this place and running Playtime over at Toyland. It'll be fine— We'll just have to make time to see each other when we can."

"Yeah…" He dragged out his comment in a doubtful tone. "That's really not gonna work for me."

Taken aback by his reaction, she quickly came up with a suggestion. "Then I can help you with your studying. I didn't learn much useful stuff in college, but I did really well in my classes, and I even worked at the campus tutoring center. I can help you come up with lesson plans and go over material with you. If you want, I'll quiz you to make sure you've got it all straight."

As her voice rose in pitch and speed, Lauren was well aware that she was beginning to sound desperate. Which made sense, because she was heading in that general direction. To have Ben stay in town, only to lose him to a demanding job ten miles away, would be worse than him being in Boston. At least then she wouldn't expect to see him, so missing him would eventually become something she learned to live with.

"It's nice of you to offer, but that's not quite what I had in mind." A frown lined his mouth, but the corner of it suddenly twitched with something less somber, and she couldn't imagine what was going on in his head. She didn't have to wait long for an explanation.

While she watched in disbelief, he went down on one knee and stared up at her with raw, unabashed emotion shining in his eyes. She was so astonished, it took her a few moments to notice the diamond ring sparkling in the late-afternoon sun.

It was a good thing he began to talk, because she couldn't have spoken properly if she tried.

"Lauren, we've been through a lot these past

few months, on our own and together. Not long ago I realized that sharing things with you—good or bad—is a lot better than being stubborn and trying to handle them by myself. I love you more than I can ever say, and I'm really hoping you'll marry me."

She'd recovered enough to come up with a response, and she couldn't help teasing this incredible man who'd brought the light back into her life. "That's not a question."

Chuckling, he stood and took her left hand. Meeting her gaze, he asked, "Lauren, will you be my wife and come build a future with me?"

"Yes and yes." As she watched him slide the ring onto her finger, she marveled at how perfect the modest setting he'd chosen looked on her hand. In the past, she'd had much more glamorous jewelry, but all those pieces paled in comparison to this one. Because it had come from Ben, she'd treasure it forever.

"One more question." Looking up, she nodded and he went on. "I know it's really sudden, but how would you feel about a September wedding?"

At first, she didn't understand the rush, but she quickly caught on. "You mean, before the restoration starts?"

"There's a lot to do, and it's gonna be one of those 24/7 kinda jobs for a while. If you're good with it, I'd really like for us to be married before the on-site work starts."

"Oh, I'm good with it," she assured him with a delighted kiss. "I'm very good with it."

* * * * *

Dear Reader,

As the opening verse says, this story is about finding light in the darkness. It's about accepting what happened to us in the past and moving on to create a better future. Sometimes that means literally running away, as Lauren did, or staying put and molding things into a better shape, as Ben chose to do. Either way, the key is to choose a new path and follow where it leads. Easier said than done, to be sure.

We all have things in our personal histories we're not crazy about. As Lauren and Ben learned, those things may have helped form us, but they don't define us. Because we're human, we're always evolving and nothing is set in stone until we stop trying to change our circumstances. With determination, we can overcome painful memories and use them as a foundation to build a better, more positive life for ourselves and the people we love.

If you'd like to stop by for a visit, you'll find me online at www.miaross.com, Facebook and Twitter. While you're there, send me a message in your favorite format. I'd love to hear from you!

Mia Ross

Questions for Discussion

1. When the story opens, all Lauren wants is to feel safe again. Have you or someone you know experienced something like this?

2. Because of her wariness around him, Ben quickly realizes Lauren was in an abusive relationship. Rather than pulling back, he encourages her to trust him and helps her regain her confidence. If you met someone like Lauren, how would you handle the situation?

3. Lauren's mother is a social worker, and her father's a police detective. Because of that, she's worried about their reaction and doesn't tell them about Jeremy's abusive behavior. Do you think she did the right thing?

4. Ben's parents had a tumultuous marriage that shapes his views on relationships. Do you or someone you know feel the same way? How have you handled it?

5. Even Ben's strong faith couldn't prepare him for the disintegration of his family,

but it did help him soldier on when things got tough. Has anything like this ever happened to you? How did your faith help you through it?

6. The close-knit, caring community in Holiday Harbor appeals to Lauren, and she gradually comes out of her shell. Do you know someone who seems closed-off this way? If so, what could you do to help draw them out?

7. For Lauren, regular worship is a distant memory. At the Safe Harbor Church, she finds a warm, vibrant group of people who make her feel welcome, and she enjoys attending services with them. What is it about your church that you like the most?

8. Different as they seem to be, Ben and Lauren share a reverence for history that brings them together. Can opposites really attract, or do you think a successful relationship requires people to have many things in common?

9. In her new job at Toyland, Lauren discovers that despite studying business in college, she loves working with kids. Have

you had the opportunity to make a similar change in your own life? If so, what was the result?

10. The Easter egg hunt is a long-standing town event, but this year the kids involved color the eggs for hiding. Can you think of new ways to celebrate traditional holidays in your town?

11. For years, Ben has longed to leave his hometown and work on challenging historical preservation sites. When he's forced to choose between his dream job and remaining in Holiday Harbor with Lauren, he follows his heart and stays to be with her. Have you ever faced a similar choice? If so, what did you decide?

12. When Ben turns down a plum job in Boston, a landmark project opens up in a nearby town, and he signs onto the crew. He takes this to be God's way of rewarding him for making the right choice. Have you ever been in a similar situation? If so, what happened?

LARGER-PRINT BOOKS!

**GET 2 FREE
LARGER-PRINT NOVELS
PLUS 2 FREE
MYSTERY GIFTS**

Love Inspired

Larger-print novels are now available...

YES! Please send me 2 FREE LARGER-PRINT Love Inspired® novels and my 2 FREE mystery gifts (gifts are worth about $10). After receiving them, if I don't wish to receive any more books, I can return the shipping statement marked "cancel." If I don't cancel, I will receive 6 brand-new novels every month and be billed just $5.24 per book in the U.S. or $5.74 per book in Canada. That's a savings of at least 23% off the cover price. It's quite a bargain! Shipping and handling is just 50¢ per book in the U.S. and 75¢ per book in Canada.* I understand that accepting the 2 free books and gifts places me under no obligation to buy anything. I can always return a shipment and cancel at any time. Even if I never buy another book, the two free books and gifts are mine to keep forever.

122/322 IDN F49Y

Name	(PLEASE PRINT)

Address	Apt. #

City	State/Prov.	Zip/Postal Code

Signature (if under 18, a parent or guardian must sign)

Mail to the **Harlequin® Reader Service:**
IN U.S.A.: P.O. Box 1867, Buffalo, NY 14240-1867
IN CANADA: P.O. Box 609, Fort Erie, Ontario L2A 5X3

**Are you a current subscriber to Love Inspired books
and want to receive the larger-print edition?
Call 1-800-873-8635 or visit www.ReaderService.com.**

* Terms and prices subject to change without notice. Prices do not include applicable taxes. Sales tax applicable in N.Y. Canadian residents will be charged applicable taxes. Offer not valid in Quebec. This offer is limited to one order per household. Not valid for current subscribers to Love Inspired Larger-Print books. All orders subject to credit approval. Credit or debit balances in a customer's account(s) may be offset by any other outstanding balance owed by or to the customer. Please allow 4 to 6 weeks for delivery. Offer available while quantities last.

Your Privacy—The Harlequin® Reader Service is committed to protecting your privacy. Our Privacy Policy is available online at www.ReaderService.com or upon request from the Harlequin Reader Service.

We make a portion of our mailing list available to reputable third parties that offer products we believe may interest you. If you prefer that we not exchange your name with third parties, or if you wish to clarify or modify your communication preferences, please visit us at www.ReaderService.com/consumerchoice or write to us at Harlequin Reader Service Preference Service, P.O. Box 9062, Buffalo, NY 14269. Include your complete name and address.

LILPDIR13R

LARGER-PRINT BOOKS!

GET 2 FREE
LARGER-PRINT NOVELS
PLUS 2 FREE
MYSTERY GIFTS

Love Inspired
SUSPENSE
RIVETING INSPIRATIONAL ROMANCE

Larger-print novels are now available...

REQUEST YOUR FREE BOOKS!

2 FREE INSPIRATIONAL NOVELS
PLUS 2
FREE
MYSTERY GIFTS

Love Inspired.

HISTORICAL
INSPIRATIONAL HISTORICAL ROMANCE

YES! Please send me 2 FREE Love Inspired® Historical novels and my 2 FREE mystery gifts (gifts are worth about $10). After receiving them, if I don't wish to receive any more books, I can return the shipping statement marked "cancel." If I don't cancel, I will receive 4 brand-new novels every month and be billed just $4.74 per book in the U.S. or $5.24 per book in Canada. That's a savings of at least 21% off the cover price. It's quite a bargain! Shipping and handling is just 50¢ per book in the U.S. and 75¢ per book in Canada.* I understand that accepting the 2 free books and gifts places me under no obligation to buy anything. I can always return a shipment and cancel at any time. Even if I never buy another book, the two free books and gifts are mine to keep forever.

102/302 IDN F5CY

Name	(PLEASE PRINT)

Address	Apt. #

City	State/Prov.	Zip/Postal Code

Signature (if under 18, a parent or guardian must sign)

Mail to the **Harlequin® Reader Service:**
IN U.S.A.: P.O. Box 1867, Buffalo, NY 14240-1867
IN CANADA: P.O. Box 609, Fort Erie, Ontario L2A 5X3

Want to try two free books from another series?
Call 1-800-873-8635 or visit www.ReaderService.com.

* Terms and prices subject to change without notice. Prices do not include applicable taxes. Sales tax applicable in N.Y. Canadian residents will be charged applicable taxes. Offer not valid in Quebec. This offer is limited to one order per household. Not valid for current subscribers to Love Inspired Historical books. All orders subject to credit approval. Credit or debit balances in a customer's account(s) may be offset by any other outstanding balance owed by or to the customer. Please allow 4 to 6 weeks for delivery. Offer available while quantities last.

Your Privacy—The Harlequin® Reader Service is committed to protecting your privacy. Our Privacy Policy is available online at www.ReaderService.com or upon request from the Harlequin Reader Service.

We make a portion of our mailing list available to reputable third parties that offer products we believe may interest you. If you prefer that we not exchange your name with third parties, or if you wish to clarify or modify your communication preferences, please visit us at www.ReaderService.com/consumerschoice or write to us at Harlequin Reader Service Preference Service, P.O. Box 9062, Buffalo, NY 14269. Include your complete name and address.

ReaderService.com

Manage your account online!
- Review your order history
- Manage your payments
- Update your address

Enjoy all the features!
- Reader excerpts from any series
- Respond to mailings and special monthly offers
- Discover new series available to you
- Browse the Bonus Bucks catalog
- Share your feedback

Visit us at:
ReaderService.com

RS13